THE
MIDNIGHT BOAT
TO
PALERMO
And Other Stories

ROSEMARY AUBERT

THE MIDNIGHT BOAT TO PALERMO

and other stories

Rosemary Aubert

ISBN: 978-1-77242-045-6

CARRICK
PUBLISHING

Print Edition

Carrick Publishing

www.carrickpublishing.com

Cover Art by Douglas Purdon

Cover Design by Sara Carrick

TABLE OF CONTENTS

Waiting for My Brother	1
Getting Rid of Cottage Pests	19
The Thief	25
Shaving with Occam's Razor	39
On the Job	47
Water Like a Stone	55
Gifts	67
Old Maids	75
The Bench Rests	83
The Biker and the Butter	99
Safe Water	111
The Toy	119
Merry Christmas, Dear Orphans	125
Taking Off	131
The Canadian Caper	141
The Prime Suspect	151
The Midnight Boat to Palermo	159
About the Author	173

Publication Credits

The following stories have been previously published:

"Getting Rid of Cottage Pests": *Cottage Country Killers*, eds.: Vicki Cameron and Linda Wiken, Burnstown, ON, General Store Publishing House, 1997.

"The Thief": Second place winner, Bloody Pete Awards, 2006 Bloody Words Conference. Published in conference program booklet.

Also published in *Big Pond Rumours ezine*, summer 2016

"Shaving with Occam's Razor": *Bloody York*, ed: David Skene-Melvin, Simon & Pierre, 1996.

"Water Like a Stone": *Blood on the Holly*, ed: Caro Soles, Baskerville Books, 2007.

"Gifts": *Over the Edge*, eds: Peter Sellers and Robert J. Sawyer, Pottersfield Press, 2000.

"The Bench Rests": *13 O'Clock*, ed: Donna Carrick, Carrick Publishing, 2015.

"The Canadian Caper": *Thirteen*, eds: M.H. Callway, Donna Carrick, Joan O'Callaghan, Carrick Publishing, 2013.

"The Prime Suspect": *World Enough and Crime*, eds: Donna & Alex Carrick, Carrick Publishing and Excerpt Flight Deck, 2014.

"The Midnight Boat to Palermo": *Cold Blood V*, ed: Peter Sellers, Mosaic, 1994. Reprinted *Les Prix Arthur-Ellis-1*, ed: Peter Sellers, Editions Alive Inc., 2003.

This book is dedicated to my beloved husband, Douglas Purdon.

WAITING FOR MY BROTHER

Every day for the past four I'd had to wake up to the same yelling and screaming. Out on the street, the cops were harassing me again and I had to lie low. Keeping off the street meant no work. No work meant no rent. No rent meant the landlady blasting away outside my door. First her voice. Then her fists.

I could hear banging even when I was dead asleep, but I couldn't risk yelling back. There was always an outside chance it could be the police.

Whoever it was got lost when they got no answer. I turned over and snuggled deeper into the sheets. I couldn't remember how many months it'd been since I wrapped them around an old mattress from the hallway. My brother had taught me how to look for things to use and how to take them—even something big like a mattress—before anybody knew they were missing.

I'd just settled nicely back into a dream when I heard another sound. About an inch from my nose, a cockroach was working over a crumb on the floor. I found a book and squished the cockroach. I wiped the book by dragging it across the sheet. Then I went back to sleep.

In a little while, I woke up again. I kept getting pains in my stomach. Sleeping instead of eating was something else my brother had taught me, but it had its limits. I was starving; I had no cash. I got up, threw on a t-shirt and jeans and headed down to the shelter.

The walls were peeling. The floors were stained and cracked. But the thing I hated worst there was the smell. Of dirty people with filthy clothes smoking raggedy roll-your-owns and drinking coffee burned down to the tarry bottom of the pot. The smell of glue, cough medicine, bleach and all the other cheap things losers get high on.

I wasn't crazy about the losers themselves, either. For starters, they were all old—nothing but a bunch of ancient ragbags waiting for a handout. And pushy. "Too late, sweets," some geezer said as he reached in front of me for the last squashed cinnamon roll on a dented foil tray. It was so hot in there all the time. But the old guy wore a thick hunter's sweater with deer on it. There were big holes under each arm, probably because the sweater was about three sizes too small.

I managed to grab a hard bun and a cup of lukewarm coffee. I was almost finished when I glanced up and saw my least favorite fruitcake coming right at me.

I didn't know what had set her off, but from the first day she ever saw me, she never let me alone. Like she was my guardian angel—or devil. She'd been following me around for almost as long as the Prince had been gone. I stood up to get away, but I wasn't fast enough. She stared at me like with the evil eye. I sat back down.

There was something different about her today. Her eyes were clear—almost like a normal person. When she opened her mouth and started to talk, I was shocked. I never heard her talk before.

She reached out and touched my leg. I could feel the bony fingers right through my jeans. Like I said, it was a hot morning, but the hair on my arms was standing up.

She said, "The Prince is coming down."

"What? What did you say?"

"What's said is said...." She clamped her jaw and turned to my coffee, picking it up in shaky, old-lady jerks. I

2

felt like smacking her hand and making her spill it all over herself, but I had to calm down.

"Look," I said, "I'm sorry I shoot my mouth off at you all the time. I just feel a little funny when somebody follows me, you know?"

She kept slurping the coffee. "Come on, just tell me what you know about the Prince. Please—"

I waited while she lifted the cup again, gulped, then took a really long time putting it back down on the table. I couldn't take it anymore. "Come on, you old hag, what do you know about the Prince?" I grabbed her shoulder and gave it a good shake.

She looked up, confused, afraid. It was like she'd never seen me before in her life. Then her eyes glazed over.

Nothing. All the lights out. Nobody home.

"You old witch!" I yelled, raising my fist. "You stupid old useless hag—"

Before two seconds passed there were five old geezers on me pounding away at my back and my arms and even giving me a couple of weak kicks on my shins and calves.

It made me laugh more than it hurt, but I figured my welcome must be about worn out.

All day I thought about what the old bag lady had said. "The Prince is coming down." Could it be true? Did he get off?

Maybe he escaped. Maybe this news meant the Prince was in it worse than ever, but I couldn't help smiling. I missed him. I needed him. He was a major pain, of course. So who wasn't? At least when the Prince was around, I had somebody to talk to.

Four days shot and the super bugging me every day. Maybe if the Prince was really back, he could help me out with the rent. But until then, I had to work, cops or no cops.

The action was slow on the Track. It took all afternoon and half the bloody night to get the money for two weeks' rent. And I was only able to do it because I'd rested for four days.

When I finally got enough, I stuffed the money in an envelope I found blowing around on the sidewalk. Then I went home, washed my face, changed out of my working clothes and knocked on the landlady's door.

It wasn't until I'd handed the witch the envelope that it occurred to me I hadn't left any out for myself. And I was starving again. I'd had nothing but cigarettes and Coke since breakfast. I decided to go back out and see if I could score some food.

I'd about had my fill of drop-in centers after the mess at breakfast. I tried to think of somebody who owed me, but there wasn't anybody left. If I'd had drugs to trade, I could have gotten something to eat in a second. But I was right out of them, too. I could steal off an outdoor stand or shoplift. But with the cops after me already, I didn't want to try that just then.

I was considering checking out some restaurant garbage cans when I got lucky.

I was walking along Yonge Street near the Eaton Centre, not really paying attention to the action, when I saw a familiar shape bump and slide and scrape across the sidewalk—Hipbone the smashed-up paper seller going for coffee!

I followed him with my eyes as he moved past a crowd of people gathered on the corner listening to a religious guy preach his lungs out.

4

As soon as Hipbone got to a point where the crowd of people was between him and me, I moved. I took my time easing up to the big metal newspaper box that opened at the top to form a stand. Like other paper sellers on Yonge, Hipbone had built himself quite a little fortress. In front of the stand he had a milk crate with a shaggy old pillow on it for a seat and a couple other crates piled up so that when he sat down, he was protected on three sides—like a grungy old executive in an office.

A dumb executive. In the open part of the stand on top of the piles of newspapers was a metal scoop. Amazing as it was, he trusted people to put coins in there when he wasn't minding the stall. Even more amazing—most people did it. And nobody touched the coins.

Until now.

As the crowd moved closer to the preacher promising them eternal burning in the fires of hell, I emptied the scoop into my pocket—just before Hipbone reappeared with a big Styrofoam cup dribbling coffee down the front of his already-stained pants.

Making as if I'd just arrived on the scene, I sidled up and wormed my way toward the front of the crowd. It was as good a way to fool Hipbone as any.

But when he started screaming as loud as his scratchy old voice could manage, "Hypocrites! Listening to a sermon about Jesus! Robbers!" I felt guilty. In fact, I almost felt like crying. *Don't take from your own, unless you can't help it.* That was one of the Prince's rules. Like honor among thieves or something.

Some people started yelling at Hipbone to shut up…. Then others started to yell at *them* to shut up. Out of the corner of my eye, I saw a police cruiser. I pushed my way back toward the street.

But Hipbone saw me. He called, "Brianna—hey... Wait! Listen to this...."

He kept calling and I kept pushing until I got too far away to hear him or for him to catch me. I slowed down, trying to look cool, so nobody could see I was really running away.

I ducked across the street into a shopping mall and didn't come out until I was a block away from the mess. It wasn't until my heart stopped pounding that I realized what Hipbone was yelling to me. He wasn't telling me to stop. He didn't realize I was the sleaze who took his money. He was telling me something. Suddenly I realized what he'd been saying. "Brianna, the Prince is back...."

I needed to think. I had plenty of coins and I felt like my stomach was totally empty. So I slipped into a nearby pizza place and grabbed a large Coke and two slices of all-dressed. As I ate, I watched the street. A couple cruisers went by, headed in the direction of Hipbone's corner. I hadn't meant to cause so much trouble.

After a while, though, I stopped looking beyond the window and started looking at it. I could see my reflection in the slimy glass. I knew everybody thought I was ugly, though once in a while some stupid John would squeeze out that I was beautiful. Perverts.

But my looks didn't stop people hassling me. Four years of fighting off pimps by day and weirdos by night. I had to smile. I figured with the Prince back, everybody else on the street, pimps included, would leave me alone.

Thinking about that, I touched my scar. I could see it in the reflection—a white line from the corner of my eye to the tip of my chin. I still remembered the night it happened, the sound of the blade cutting my skin, and the Prince crying afterward and telling me how sorry he was that he hurt me.

Then he said as long as I was working for him at least I knew I wouldn't get hurt from a pimp who was a stranger. We both had to laugh at that.

Out on the street things were back to normal. Whatever had happened with Hipbone was over—and I still had a lot of coin. I walked past the flashing lights of camera stores and computer discounts. The light was so bright you could see the bums sleeping in the doorways, curled up like big, dirty babies.

The roar of the games arcade hit me the minute I yanked open the door—the shouts of people playing combined with silly, jittery electronic tunes, fake gunshots, bombs, machine-gun fire, the noise of computer helicopters and motorcycles, race cars. Spaceships. Stupid and cool.

All of a sudden, I felt like dancing in between the wall-to-wall people—mostly young guys in jeans or leather—all with their eyes on the machines and their backs to each other, everybody alive, in motion, jumping and yelling.

I followed a long row of flashing red and blue bulbs until I got to my favorite—the Amazon pinball. It was painted with a beautiful woman dressed only in flowers, holding a strong bow with a wicked arrow.

I slipped in a couple of twonies and pressed a button for the ball to come up. Then I yanked back the plunger. I let my fingers feel it up for a second or two, holding back hard against the spring. I let it go a little, then pulled back on it as hard as I could and let it fly, the cool metal sliding against my thumb.

Right away, I jammed my fingers against the flipper buttons, waiting for the ball to whizz through the bright orange, purple, yellow, blue, red flowers all over the board. The ball was an Amazon in the jungle—and every time I gave it a good smack with the flippers, it went flying up the board to ding and rattle and ping like a song.

I lost track of the twonies, and I lost track of the time. I was so far gone that when I looked up and saw I wasn't alone at the machine, I jumped.

Handy Randy was okay, even if he was a skinny, pink-and-white haired little punk from boystown who wrote poems for a hobby. He thought he looked like an adult, of course, but I figured him for fourteen at the most.

"Hey, there, Rand—" I said, taking my eyes from the game only for a second. "How's it going, lady?"

"I got a message," Randy said mysteriously.

"Yeah, really?" I watched a lazy ball hit a couple of bells before meandering down toward the flippers. "Like what?"

"It's about the Prince."

"What?" I had to look right at him. While my ball took a nice little shooteroo right down the tube.

"The Prince—"

"Did you talk to him?"

"Yeah, maybe I did—" Randy said with a self-satisfied smile.

"What did he say? Is he around?" I leaned closer to the kid. He smelled like a drugstore perfume counter. "Come on, Randy, don't hold out on me."

"Okay, okay. I saw the Prince and he wants to see you—"

"Where is he?"

"I don't know—"

"Oh come on, Randy, please—" Out of the corner of my eye, I saw one of the bouncers approaching. The rule is play or get out. "What's the message? Spit it out—"

"The Prince says tomorrow. Fraser. At two."

"What? What's that supposed to mean?"

"I don't know. You got to figure it out—"

"Come on, Randy, this isn't a game...."

"Look, Bri, that's all I know, okay?"

"You swear?"

"Yeah. Just figure it out. I can't hang around. I got a customer waiting."

He took off. It was no use trying to follow him through the video zoo. I went back to the machine.

But I couldn't concentrate. I checked out the clock beside the huge sci-fi painting somebody had done on the wall long enough ago for it to be half dust and half paint. It was five minutes to midnight. Tomorrow at two could be as close as two hours and five minutes from now.

I knew what Fraser was. In the beginning, after I ran away just by taking transit out of the stupid suburbs, the Prince was teaching me things. We spent a couple of weeks on Fraser Street—and we would have squatted there forever if the cops hadn't chased us because some arty type from one of the studios complained.

I pushed my way through the video crowd, using my elbows when I had to. One or two guys yelled, but I ignored them.

Out on the street, some idiots were filming a movie. They had cables and lights and jerks with clipboards all over the place. I ducked into the shadows fast. Only a total loser stands still for a camera. Parents, cops and social workers watch everything. A person is a fool to take a chance. Even a person like me who has no family looking for them.

Except the Prince.

I shoved the last of my change into the fare box. Lucky for me, the driver couldn't count. I yanked a transfer out of her hand and pushed my way through the crowd of late-night losers right to the back of the bus where I slid down into the last seat left.

The vomit comet bumped along Yonge Street picking up stray drunks, loud kids, cleaning ladies. At King, I jumped off and used my transfer to grab a streetcar west.

By the time I got off at Dufferin, the streets were starting to get that empty look they have when all the straight people have gone home to bed. There was nobody in sight except for a bag lady asleep in a doorway.

The woman opened her eyes and I got a familiar creepy feeling. This wasn't any old hag—it was my guardian looney, the old witch that seemed to follow me everywhere. I turned off King and onto Fraser as fast as I could.

One side of the street was nothing but a huge open stadium. Across the empty playing field I could see a big blue sign flashing in the distance. The sight of it made me laugh, made me remember the summer night the Prince and I, stoned out on a little something I'd scored off a trick, had lain on the grass of the field and tried to shout "on" and "off" in time to the sign—like it was us making it work instead of some dumb computer somewhere.

There was another set of lights in the distance—the gold and blue dome of one of the buildings of the Exhibition grounds. My memory of that went farther back—to the time my father used to take me to the fair every summer. He told me fairies lived in domes, flying around the top where nobody could see them. Of course—like a stupid idiot—I believed him.

The other side of Fraser was different. From the sidewalk, the whole block looked like one long building, six floors high. But as soon as I found what I was looking for—a narrow alley lit by a dusty old bulb in an iron cage—and slipped through it, I was in a whole different city—just like in the Dickens books I lifted from the library once in a while.

Here there were all kinds of old warehouses and office buildings from a hundred years ago—still in perfect shape. Some were set around a sort of courtyard in the middle, others on narrow streets. There were iron fire escapes with little balconies and metal loading doors with huge bolts and hinges. Most of the buildings had high windows with hundreds of tiny panes under curved tops like the windows of a palace or a church.

The place seemed deserted, but it wasn't really. Even though the buildings were mostly dark, almost every one of them had a light shining in it somewhere. Nearby I could hear a saxophone going—and the same bunch of notes played over and over on electronic keyboard. A bright red motor scooter was parked beside a loading dock along one of the buildings, sitting there as if the owner would be back any minute.

I did a three-hundred-sixty degree turn, trying to figure out where I was supposed to go. A slight noise caught my attention. I jumped when I saw a tall, skinny, bald naked guy glancing at me over his shoulder out one of the windows way up.

Then I doubled over laughing when I realized it was just a manikin in some fashion studio.

I walked toward that building anyway, and when I got closer, I saw an open door on the first floor. Slow, listening hard for sounds from inside, I walked toward the door.

The nearer I got, the more my heart pounded. I gave the door a shove.

It creaked open on complete darkness, except for the light coming over my shoulder from outside. I could make out a hallway, and off that what seemed to be a room. Somebody was breathing in there.

My heart jumped into my mouth and I turned to run. But too late.

Before I knew what had me, a hand bunched my t-shirt so tight around my neck, I thought I was going to choke. My fingers flew up, trying to free my throat so I could breathe, trying to get the bastard off me.

Hard as I could, I brought my foot up sharp to get my heels into his shins, but the son of a bitch pulled back, taking me with him. I squirmed and elbowed and kicked, but it didn't do a bit of good. He was way stronger than me, strong enough to hold me with one hand—no matter how much I wiggled—and slam shut the door with the other.

The minute the door shut and the light was gone altogether, he let me go. It took a second to realize I was free. I reached out in the darkness. My hands hit nothing but air.

"What the hell is this?" I shouted, hating the sound of fear so clear in my voice. "Who the hell are you? What do you want?"

For answer I got nothing but the same breathing sound as before.

I stood still for a minute, trying to get my bearings in the room, but it was useless; I had no idea where I was. Or where he was—assuming it was a he.

I forced my heart to stop pounding, forced myself to think. As long as it was pitch dark, the only advantage he had over me was physical strength. So what? I wasn't what I was for nothing. I'd gotten the better of customers bigger and stronger than myself lots of times. All I had to do was stay cool....

I kept as still as I could, trying to judge what direction the sound of his breathing came from. He seemed to be moving all around me, circling me like a dog circles a rat. I didn't move. Just the way rats don't. I knew if I could figure out a pattern to his motions, I could jump him.

He jumped me first. I felt the full weight of his body hit me at once, tumbling us both to the floor, his arms locked around me breaking my fall, as if he didn't want me to get hurt.

And then I heard his soft, familiar laugh in my ear and felt him kiss my cheek and tighten his arms in a hug.

"Jamie, you idiot, what the hell are you trying to prove—you stupid bucket of…"

I was crying and laughing and pushing him away and pulling him toward me all at the same time—still not able to see a damn thing or hear anything but my own words.

He laughed again. "So you got the message…."

"Yeah, I got the message. Messages. Who's that old spook of a bag lady who follows me all the time, anyway?"

"One of my other girls— You jealous, Bri?" He touched my face with the back of his hand. "You think you're the only one I love?"

It made me furious when he teased me like that. I was glad it was dark. The Prince had hit me for having the wrong look on my face before this. And the wrong tone in my voice. I had to wait a minute before I said, "So are we going to sit here in the dark all night or are you going to stop playing around and turn on the light?"

"Prince of darkness, that's what I am!" he said.

"That's the devil," I answered. "And you're not that—"

"Some people would disagree," he answered, without any particular emotion. I felt him move away, and I just sat there waiting for whatever he decided to do next.

"Well, Brianna," he finally said, "what do you think? You want to see what the Prince is looking like these days?

You want to see what a couple of years of time does to a guy?"

All of a sudden I was scared again. Scared in a worse way than when he'd grabbed me. When he'd gone up, Jamie had been sixteen, the best-looking guy on the Track. He'd been in a lot of fights, but he didn't have a mark on him. And no tattoos, either. I had plenty of tattoos myself, so I didn't give a damn. It was just that the Prince was perfect looking. My mother said he was perfect looking from the time we were born.

"What do you mean? Did you get cut or something?"

"Of course I got cut. You think I'm going to do time and not get cut?"

"Jamie, I don't want—"

Before I could finish, the room was all of a sudden filled with light. It was a little room, looking like it was just finished being renovated. It was painted all white. It was completely empty, so that the only thing there was to look at was the Prince.

He was taller than he'd been when he went away—much taller than me and I'm not short. His legs looked strong in jeans that were tight enough but too new. Since I was sitting on the floor at his feet, I could see that his boots were new, too. Like the jail gave him some kind of clothes allowance or something.

But his leather jacket I'd seen before. It was scuffed and scratched from a hundred street fights. The sight of it filled my heart with happiness. Slowly I let my eyes move up toward his face.

There still wasn't a mark on him. His good, tough, square jaw was as proud as ever and his eyes danced the same way they always did, like there was something going on there that nobody would ever be able to guess.

The guards hadn't cut his hair, either. It was even longer than before. The bright light made it shine as it fell in a heap of curls from his forehead to his big shoulders.

He was beautiful! As beautiful as the prince in any story. I was so happy to see him, I thought my heart would explode.

I jumped up and grabbed him, standing on my toes and trying to get my arms around him—not easy because he was a lot bigger than me. Except for the occasional old customer who missed his wife or kid and was willing to pay for the privilege, I hadn't hugged anybody in a long time. It felt like heaven. "Oh, Jamie, don't go away again. Don't get in trouble again—"

The Prince pulled away. He smiled. He leaned back against the wall, one foot up against the whiteness. He dug in his pocket for makings and rolled a joint for himself, sucking in hard and holding his breath as he passed it to me.

I shook my head. I needed to keep my thoughts clear because I knew what was coming next.

"Business been okay?" he asked

"Not bad."

"Those cops still on your butt?"

"No. Guess they got bigger fish to fry or something…." I lied.

"How much you pulling in a night?"

"I guess that recession thing sort of hit people—"

He took another drag on the joint. "That's not what I asked, is it?" The tone of his voice reminded me I better be careful.

I glanced down. There was an ugly black mark from his boot on the perfect white wall. My voice felt stuck in my throat.

"Come on—spit it out…."

"I'm older now. I don't get as much as I used to, Jamie, and everything's really gone up. I pay rent, I—"

He took the cloth of my t-shirt between his fingers and gave it a little twist. "Sounds like you need me—am I right?"

"I don't want you to hurt me, Jamie. I'm done with that—"

"Well, hurting you's not what I want, either." He shoved me away, but he kept his eyes on mine. I could see the anger melting away. That was a good thing about Jamie. He got mad strong but not for long.

"Look, Bri," he said, again leaning on the wall, "you got to help me out here. I been up for almost two. I'm gonna need a place to stay. You're family. I gotta count on you...."

"I know."

"So you gotta, you know, share. Maybe work a little harder."

"Okay."

"Good," he said, touching my face, "I'm glad we talked about that." He sucked up the last smoke from the joint and tossed it onto the floor where it burned a little circle in the shiny wood before it went out.

"You want to go for a ride?" he asked.

"A ride? Where?"

"Any place. You see that motor scooter out there?"

"Yeah. Is it yours?"

"Not yet. But it can be if you want. What do you say? We can go down to the harbor and stone a few gulls."

"You're crazy, Jamie. You wouldn't do that!"

"No. Wouldn't be any fun. They're all asleep. Sitting ducks. Gulls."

We burst into a fit of giggles. "Sure," I said, "what the hell? Let's."

"Right! Come on!"

He took my hand and led me out of the building, the two of us clowning around, sneaking on tiptoes and holding our fingers to our lips as if to warn each other to be quiet. It was a hoot. Just like old times.

I was so happy I could sing. He started the scooter—Jamie could get anything going, key or no key—and we took off. By the time the fool who owned the thing discovered it was gone, we'd be miles away.

It was so good to have the Prince back. I put my arms around his waist and laid my head on the scuffed back of his jacket that smelled like cigs and sweat and trouble and fun.

The bike tore through the dark empty streets, the sound of it making an echo off the buildings. The wind hit my face—it hurt and felt good at the same time. Like a slap. Like a kiss.

GETTING RID OF COTTAGE PESTS

When I first started going up to the cottage, I hated how you had to be killing something—or thinking about killing something—all the time.

I guess the first time I noticed was with the garden. My husband said that if I was going to learn to love the country, there was no better way to begin than gardening. "You'll enjoy it," he said, "it'll be just like the balcony…."

Only it wasn't. The impatiens and pansies in the window boxes on the balcony of our high-rise apartment were delicate and lovely. The garden at the cottage was overrun with weeds—some of them as big as I am. I particularly hated one that was tall and thick but with a single tiny flower at the top. Like a large man with a small head.

I pulled and tugged and whacked and felt that the plants were far stronger than I. But in the end, I had a large pile of dead ones.

"Good girl," my husband said. Then he handed me a rake and a hoe. I was tired, but he said that country life was about endurance and that a city person like me could use a little more of what he called "stamina."

It was then that I realized how many creatures have been killed in the name of gardening. My rake, grabbing clumps of thick, brown dirt, scraped across a nest of beetles. As shocked as I would have been had the roof of the cottage suddenly flown away, I watched as they scrambled in all directions, disappearing under the black clods I'd displaced.

I shuddered. My husband, watching from beside the stump of a tree he'd just felled to let more light into the

19

garden, laughed. "That's it," he said, "get 'em running. The more bugs you chase out of there, the better."

Luckily, he had gone to wash up and wasn't there when my hoe cut a worm in half and I burst into tears. I brushed the earth back over the halves and went in to cook supper.

The garden wasn't much of a success. Even though my husband sprayed everything with what he called "a damn good dose" of insecticide, every weekend when I went to look at the spindly plants, there were bites out of the leaves.

"Animals," my husband said. He took me by the hand and walked me around the garden. "You're not paying attention," he announced. "Look at this—"

I didn't know what he was looking at, but he put his hand at the back of my neck and bent my head until my eyes were trained on the dirt at my feet. I saw a little hole, about the size of a dollar coin. "Baby chipmunks...."

"Oh!" I cried in delight. I leaned down toward the hole, but before I could catch a glimpse of the babies, my husband grabbed a handful of soil and shoved it into the opening. "That'll fix the little bastards," he said.

As the weeks went on, the window boxes in the city thrived. Sometimes we'd eat breakfast on the balcony, looking out over the city, so calm and peaceful in the early morning haze of summer.

Come Friday, though, it would be back to cottage country.

I guess it must have been about the end of July that I looked out the window after serving lunch and saw that something was swimming in the river that ran past the picture windows of the cottage. It was moving steadily and quickly, making a V in the water so wide that it reached the bank on either side.

"Beavers," my husband told me.

"How beautiful—"

"You won't say that when they start chomping on the timbers of the house—"

I laughed. I thought it was a cute joke. Then I caught a glimpse of my husband's face. Remembering the scowl on it, I wasn't surprised when, that afternoon, he made a deal with a local farmer to put traps under the water along the shore of the river. "I told him he can keep any pelt that he catches. That's what I love about the country," my husband mused, "tradition. There's still people around who know where to sell a good beaver pelt."

I started to cry. My husband took me in his arms. He ran his hands along my hair, then my cheek, wiping away the tears. "You're a typical city girl," he said, "and I find that sweet. But you have to be tough in this world. It's us against them. *Mano a mano.* You can't feel sorry for the enemy...."

When we got back home to the city, he brought me a present, a tiny orange kitten with a sweet pink nose, a little pink tongue and eyes still the blue of baby eyes. "You can bring her up to the cottage every weekend to keep you company. In fact," my husband said with a smile, "you can bring her on vacation—"

"Vacation?"

"Yes. I've arranged for us to spend the whole month of August at the cottage."

I named my kitten Baby, and it was lucky I had her or I would have died of boredom. It wasn't until we were up at the cottage day after day that I noticed there weren't any neighbours around. And the only town—about an hour away—didn't hold any interest for my husband. "And you wouldn't like it, either," he told me. "You're happier just staying here at the cottage. My little woman's turning into a country girl. I can tell."

The only trouble with Baby was that she kept trying to escape. Every time I opened the door, she ran out. Because she was so little, it wasn't hard to catch her. But after only a month, she'd doubled in size, and it seemed as if her running speed increased daily.

It was about two days before we were supposed to head back home that Baby scooted away and disappeared behind the cottage. I went running after her.

"Come back here," my husband shouted. "It's dangerous out there. Don't go off alone."

I ignored him. I wanted my kitten, my companion. I ran and ran. Behind our cottage was a ridge of rock covered with thick vegetation. Vines sucked at my ankles, but I scrambled up the hard surface after Baby. I just kept climbing. Behind me, my husband gave up shouting. I heard the door of the cottage slam once, then slam again.

I was out of breath when I finally caught up with Baby. And my heart was pounding. But when I saw what she was doing, I stopped breathing altogether.

She was standing in a clearing on top of the rock ridge. Every hair on her little body was standing on end. Her back was arched. She was hissing. She was hissing at a wolf. *Mano a mano.*

I don't know what either of them intended. Because before I could move, I heard a loud crack and saw the wolf explode in a cloud of misty red and black fuzz.

I heard two screaming sounds intertwined—the cat sound of Baby, who had jumped into my arms, and the human sound of me.

Then I heard another human sound. A laugh.

I turned. My husband was standing at the base of the rock ridge with a long-barrelled gun in his hand.

That night, I was too upset to cook supper. So my husband took me to a restaurant. I had a hard time eating, but he covered my hand with his and told me that if I was good and got down my whole supper, he would tell me about a surprise he had for me when we got home.

So I tried and I didn't do too badly.

When we got home he told me that the surprise was that he had given notice on our apartment in the city and made arrangements to have all our belongings moved to the cottage.

"We can be happy here alone and together," he whispered as we lay in bed. "And you'll toughen up a bit. You'll learn that when something is your enemy, you have to defeat it. You can't be soft. If you're afraid of your enemy, you can never sleep at night. But if you know you can kill it, you'll always be safe."

He fell asleep right after that. It had been a long hard day, after all.

At first, I cried. I thought about all the meals I'd have to cook and serve to him. Then I thought about the insecticide he'd used on the garden.

I cried some more. But my heart wasn't in it. Because I remembered how eager the trapper had been to lay traps in the woods as well as along the river bank. Maybe I could make a deal with him, too.

Also, I had seen where my husband put the gun with the long barrel.

I listened to the deep, even sound of his breathing, and suddenly, I *did* feel safe. I realized he was right. You can't feel sorry for your enemy.

At first, when I came to the cottage, I couldn't stand how you had to be killing something or thinking about killing something all the time. But as I sank into sleep, it occurred to me that after a while, it doesn't bother you at all.

THE THIEF

The gym is across the street from the courthouse and the courthouse is across the street from the cop shop. Around the corner is the detention center where a thousand people visiting their bad relatives park all day every day for free, unlike the hospital up at McCowan and Lawrence, where it'll cost you twenty bucks an hour to visit somebody who's sick.

I wouldn't be in the gym at all if it weren't for Scott— the wife. I got a hundred and twenty pounds on her. She says she doesn't want me to roll over one night and flatten her.

She doesn't want me around the house any more than I been around the house for the past twelve years.

Which is how long we've been married. As for the badge, I carried that for forty-one years. Right up until I retired a couple months ago. I wasn't a numbers man then, and I didn't need a map to tell me what part of the city I was in, let alone what part of the neighborhood. But things around here are changing fast, and changing fastest is me.

"We're delighted that you'd like to join us. And we have a special on this month. Your spouse can join for only one-half of what you pay. You can get a card and she gets her own card. You can come separately or together…. Your choice."

Yeah, right. As if Scott would hang around in a gym like this. Half the people in the place are old cops and half of the other half are old, period. Scott goes to Curves. She wears a thong. She's fifty-two years old. A knockout. I'd do anything to keep her. She's wife number three and I've got ten years on her as well as all those pounds.

So I sign up and start with the treadmill.

I walk.

At first, all I'm looking at is the place where my flat feet are supposed to be down there, somewhere below the love-handles that used to anchor my gun. I'm thinking the pound that sweet gadget weighed might be the only pound I'll ever lose.

But the second or third time I come to the gym, I start looking around.

The thing about a treadmill is: there's nothing to do *but* look around. And I see that a lot of the guys—and a few of the gals, too—are people still working across the street, people who come in on their way home from the court or the police station or the jail. And I start to listen, too, and it occurs to me that a lot of what they're talking about is business. Law business.

I don't know anybody here personally, which is good because that means nobody knows me. Cops got big mouths. Lawyers, too, I think. But like everybody else in the world, they talk more freely when they think nobody's listening, and they assume that an old guy with earphones on is listening not to them, but to his music. Which is usually true. Unless you're a cop who's spent so much time eavesdropping that it comes natural to wear earphones with no music.

And that's how I started to get daily inside reports on the hottest case going on in the big courthouse downtown, the courthouse where I spent a lot of my final hours as a cop sitting around waiting to testify.

People sitting around waiting to testify was not a problem in this case. It was a gang shootout on Yonge Street, right in the heart of the shopping district and it cost the life of an innocent teenager buying her Christmas gifts.

Most of what I overheard at the gym, I'd heard a thousand times before, maybe a hundred thousand times, but

I still liked to listen to the gab about how every effort was being made to suck up to the few witnesses who might possibly come forward willingly. "We'll even give 'em a free ticket to stay in the country," one cop joked. He knew, like I knew, how many illegal immigrants found their way into the criminal justice system even after they'd been deported.

"It was a four-way," the other guy answered. "And they got two in custody. That means two perps are still out there."

"Not to mention the two hundred people on the street and in the stores when the shooting went down. Time for a little hunt and hound—dig a few of them out and get them to talk…."

Both guys—I took them for detectives—shook their heads.

"It's been a year and a half," one said with a sigh. "You'd think…"

"I don't think nothing," the other said. "Not anymore."

Maybe they kept talking, but suddenly, I got distracted by a tug on my police-issue tee-shirt. In the moment it took me to see who was bothering me, I got the absurd thought that I'd better take care of the few fragments of police clothing I still had in my possession. There'd be none to replace these souvenirs when they turned raggedy enough for Scott to confiscate them.

"Mr. Cander?"

I hated being called mister. Detective was good. Even officer. Mister was nobody, but mister was me.

"Yeah?"

Behind me, at the foot of the treadmill stood Denise. She's a trim broad, about the size of my wife without the beauty. But a nice woman. Nice enough to offer me that half-price deal the day she signed me up. Denise is the boss around here. She can get tough if she has to. I'd seen her eject a couple of young women who were having a cat-fight over the deluxe treadmill—the one that gives you your heart-rate, blood-pressure, body-mass index the minute you step on—and does a pregnancy test, too, for all I know.

"Can you step into the office, Mr. Cander," Denise said, "I need to talk to you for a minute."

She was going to ask me some sort of favor. Forty-one years of being asked to fix parking tickets, among other things, shows a cop how to read the body-language of somebody who wants something.

"Yeah, sure," I answered.

To tell the truth, nobody had talked to me as if I were a cop in months and I was starting to miss it.

Denise was a middle-aged blond. She looked like the type who had started off blond and was bound and determined to stay one until the day she died. Determination isn't a habit, it's a character trait. I wondered what I was up against.

"What can I do for you?" I asked as I took a seat across from her at her desk, which, I saw, was neat and tidy and held nothing but two sheets of paper and a statuette of a weight-lifter, labelled "Awarded to the Manager of the Year."

"We got a thief," she said. "I know you're a cop and I want you to help us catch him."

I thought about things for a minute.

"Seems to me," I said, "you gotta lot of cops around here. Why pick me? And anyway, why not call the real cops if you suspect theft?"

Denise smiled. "Exactly," she said.

"What?"

"I don't need a real cop." She glanced at me. Glanced away. "No disrespect. What I mean is, I don't want to get anybody into serious trouble. It's not a big deal. It's just, now that we got this card system, we have to account for every minute on every machine. Stealing time off an exercise machine, it's not a crime. But—"

"But you gotta account to your boss for every minute…." I didn't add, "Or you won't get to be Manager of the Year anymore."

"Yeah."

If she'd asked me to do a rinky-dink favor like this a couple of months ago, I would have told her where to shove it. Instead, I asked her, "So what exactly is going on? People sneaking in here without a card or something?"

She sat up straighter. It never ceases to amaze me how the slightest little mystery sets an ordinary person off. "I think it's more sophisticated than that. You see," she began to rhyme off her big theory as if she'd given hours of thought to the "crime", "if somebody had just stolen a card, then our records wouldn't jive. We keep track of every card and match each one up to each person as soon as they come in. We write it all down. Number of the card. Name of the person. Time they came in. Time they left…"

She glanced up at me, her dark brown eyes sparkling. "Want to see?" she asked. "Want to see our records?"

"Uh, no thanks," I answered. "Look, I don't think…"

If I'd still been on the force, I'd be working that gang case. I had no way of proving that was so, I just figured it was. I'd worked a lot of gang cases in my time, cleared a lot of them. I was a top man. Had been. Now I was reduced to listening to a blond, middle-aged Sherlock Holmes tell me about her own big "case."

"Somebody is figuring out how to use the machines without any card at all," Denise declared, as if this were the worst crime in the whole evil, ugly city.

"No!"

She looked at me hard for a minute, and I felt bad that I'd made fun of her.

"Look," she said, "I could have asked one of the other officers who use the gym, you know, somebody still on active duty, but I thought that would have been a conflict of interest." She kept her eyes down, on her hands, I thought. She had nice nails. Like Scott's.

"I'm sorry, Denise," I said sincerely. "I know you run a tight ship here. I know you don't want anybody cheating. I can respect that. What do you want me to do?" I asked, a little surprised at the sound of my own voice. Eager.

"Maybe you could just keep your eye on things," she answered.

"Sure," I said. "Sure, I'll keep my eye on things."

"Thanks," she said softly, "thanks a lot."

A pang shot through me that I didn't expect. It had been a long time since I'd been a cop on the beat. I'd forgotten how touching it was when some poor decent citizen showed gratitude to me just for doing my job. "Don't mention it," I said. "No problem."

So I got back on the treadmill and I resumed looking around.

I have to admit I envied the younger cops I could still hear talking about that big case downtown and about how the Prosecution was hampered by the lack of witnesses. "There's people right in this neighborhood who've witnessed gang violence," they said, and I knew it was true.

But it wasn't my job to worry about that anymore. I had a different case. I had to find the thief of minutes.

At first, I just went through the motions. I walked the mill, mostly day dreaming unless Denise was somewhere in the vicinity, in which case, I made a point of looking around the whole room as if I were studying every lousy machine in it.

But after a while, I got kind of interested. I noticed that even though the card system seemed a foolproof way of keeping track of who was doing what, people did a lot of things with the cards that weren't exactly kosher, so to speak.

I realized, for example, that the system itself had a lot of weaknesses.

For example, when you came in, you put your card in a little box on the counter in front of the receptionist's desk. The girl was supposed to pick up the card, record it in the book, and hand it back to you.

Only half the time, the girl was talking to somebody—some cute guy working out or, more likely to Denise, who was quite a talker.

So rather than stand there waiting for the receptionist to hand back the card, a lot of the gym users headed to the change room and just picked the card up on the way out to the machines.

A couple of times, people picked up the wrong card and didn't realize it until they'd already inserted it in a machine. Which meant that the card and the person using the machine didn't match. Of course, nobody took this very seriously. Who cared except Denise? If somebody picked up the wrong card, mostly they just waited until the machine spit it back out again, then traded cards with whoever had their card.

And of course, people forgot their cards. That necessitated sweet-talking the receptionist into using *her* card, which was sort of generic, like a master-key. Now, when the clientele is cops, lawyers and the occasional jail guard, verbal manipulation is a tool of the trade, so talking the receptionist out of following regs was a cinch for most of the people who frequented the gym.

It wasn't until the night that I finally got bored with the treadmill and decided to walk the track that I noticed the cleaning lady.

She was a black woman, heavier than anybody else in the gym, but not so heavy that she wasn't able to balance on one of those big orange balls that everybody's so crazy about. I had seen a little Korean cop, a girl about the size of a gnat, bounce around on the thing, exercising every part of her tricky little anatomy. The cleaning lady wasn't quite so agile, but she did seem determined.

Speaking of determination, Denise caught a glimpse of the woman and shot her such a look that the poor thing slid off the ball, grabbed her feather duster and headed for the free-weights as if she were going to dust them down to the last half ounce. Though the gym would be open for another hour and a half, Denise had put in her twelve hours and was on her way out.

The next night, I came a little later. By 9:30 there were only a few people left lying on their rickety backs and pushing against twenty or thirty pounds of iron with their wrinkled old feet. From the treadmill, I checked out the room. I couldn't see anybody doing anything suspicious. It seemed to me, though, that if the big time thief was active, he or she would probably be working now that the head honcho had gone home and the little receptionist was packing up the towels for the laundry guy to pick up after the front door was locked.

There were mirrors mounted on the east and west walls of the gym. On the north and south sides, the mirrors were free-standing. The track ran behind them. It occurred to me that the mirror on the north side obscured the view from every angle of the room except the north side of the track itself.

Again I left the treadmill. Again I took to the track. I started at the west side, took a slow run—which almost killed my knees—around the loop to the south and halfway up the east side. When I got to the north side, I slowed down to a walk, a silent walk.

I rounded the corner.

And I saw the cleaning lady pumping a couple of barbells that I wasn't sure I could handle myself.

She was so intent on what she was doing that she didn't even see me. At her feet was the feather duster and the grey rag she used to swipe the handles of all the machines. Her eyes were half closed. Her black curls, which I now noticed were streaked with grey, seemed to tremble with her effort. There was a fine sheen of sweat on her forehead. Her skin looked smooth in the reflected florescent light shadowed by the rear of the mirror.

As quietly as I could, I reversed direction.

Without her seeing me, I was back on the mill.

It took me about two more weeks to figure out how she was stealing the time on the machines.

I saw her hop on a treadmill just as a customer was getting off. "Don't forget your card," she said. She grabbed it, like she wanted to make sure the guy wouldn't leave it behind. But I saw her quickly double swipe it before she handed it back. That allowed her a half-hour on the machine, but she didn't risk taking it. What she did do was dust the thing with exceptional care, all the while walking. Nobody but me paid any attention.

I saw her pull the same trick on the stationary bicycle. Not to mention the abs extender. That was easy to fake because she had to sit on it to dust it under any circumstances, and you couldn't really tell whether the thing was operational unless you were standing right behind her.

Which I was. But she was so intent on her exercise that again, she didn't see me.

At home, the wife was starting to wonder why I liked the gym so much. I told her I was getting hooked on being in shape. She said she was beginning to miss me. Next day, I tried to sneak out of the house without her asking any questions.

There had been a time when I'd crawled out of bed at two in the morning in order to work some filthy undercover job that could only be done in the middle of the night. Of course, those had been winter nights, and I'd frozen my butt sitting surveillance in the frigid reaches of a suburban parking lot or on the icy fringes of Lake Ontario where the wind blew across the water to turn my breath to ice on my beard.

Scott caught me and asked, "Where the heck are *you* off to?"

"Nowhere…"

Except it wasn't nowhere. It was the gym. And my big new case. Watching the cleaning lady work out without paying the tab.

"I think I got that thief you're after," I told Denise. But I didn't tell her who. I'd worked homicide long enough to know how important motive was. Until I could figure out why the cleaner was working out so hard, I didn't want to blow her cover. I didn't have to figure out why she was working secretly. Every minute on those machines cost. The gym, dozy as it was, wasn't cheap. I'd have saved a few C-notes if I'd taken Denise up on the two-for she'd offered when I signed up.

Just about every day, I watched that cleaner steal a few minutes on the bike, a few minutes on the treadmill, a couple of bounces on the orange ball, even one or two stealthy laps around the track with free weights in both hands. It even seemed to me that I was starting to see some improvement. She wasn't sweating anymore. And she wasn't huffing and puffing, either. She even seemed to be doing a better job of the cleaning. Sometimes in order to stay on a machine, she dusted so hard and so long that she polished the darn thing to a glow.

This went on for about three weeks. A couple of times, Denise asked me how my "investigation" was going. I told her I'd have something for her soon.

But it wasn't until one morning when I finally found myself alone in the gym with the cleaning lady that I got the one piece of information I wanted. Like with so many times in my real cases, all I had to do was ask.

I saw her circling the track. I trotted up beside her. I said, "I see you working out here all the time when you think nobody's looking. Why?"

She staggered and stopped. She got a look of fear on her face that I hadn't seen in a long time. People aren't afraid of cops anymore. Maybe she was older than I thought.

"Don't get me in trouble," she said. "Please, I need this job...."

"You don't need to be working out to be able to be a cleaner," I said. I tried to sound gruff but I guess the months off the force were starting to take their toll. Anyway, I knew I didn't care about the gym losing a few bucks. I wanted to know what she was up to.

"I'm scared," she said.

I laughed but when I saw she wasn't joking, I said, "Scared of what? Of the people in this gym?"

She gave me a look like I was a lunatic. "Not actually," she said. I could see she was no longer scared of me.

Without thinking about it, I started to run, gently, like old men do, and she started to trot beside me, as if this was one more chance to get free workout time. "I hear things all day long," she said.

"What things?"

"About all those gangstas in the apartment buildings around here." She made a sweeping gesture with her hand. It didn't stop her stride. "I live around here myself. I don't wanna be some sort of sittin' duck. They come after me, I'm gonna run…."

With that, she spurted ahead of me.

It took me a whole lap around the track to catch up with her again.

I couldn't believe how fast she could sprint. I couldn't believe how fast *I* could sprint.

But in the half minute it took me to get back to her, I figured out a plan. A way to keep both her and Denise out of trouble. And a way to make myself feel that I was just a little more than a washed-out cop with nothing to do but tread rubber.

"You know the names of any of those gangstas?" I asked.

"'Course I don't," she said. "You're a cop, ain't you? Why do you think I'd know anybody's name?"

"Because I know that people aren't usually scared enough of strangers to do something about it."

She stopped, stood in front of me. "So what you gonna do? You gonna tell Denise I been sneakin' if I don't rat on people that live in my building?"

"I'm not that thick," I said, "but I think you've got a good thing going here."

"You mean this stupid job?"

"No. I mean the working out."

"What?"

"I've been watching you for weeks. When you first started, you could hardly lift ten pounds. Now you can run around the track faster than me."

She gave me a look. "That ain't saying nothing," she spat out.

"Look," I said, ignoring her display of contempt, "I'm going to make you a deal."

"I don't make deals with cops."

"I'm not a cop."

Both of us waited for a second. I was waiting for the hurt of my own words to hit me. I don't what she was waiting for. But nothing happened until she finally said, "What deal?"

"I'll make you a legit member of the gym. You can come here when you're off duty and work out whenever you want. With your own card."

"How you gonna do that?"

"I'm going to give Denise three hundred dollars. When she says the two-for deal she offers is for spouses only, I'm going to tell her that either she gives me the deal or I'm off her investigation. If she goes for it, obviously the stealing of time stops."

"You'd do that? You'd spend three hundred dollars for me to have my own card?" She thought about it for a minute. "What do I have to do?" she asked.

"You have to write a couple of names on a piece of paper. You have to leave that piece of paper on the floor near the locker of one of those young cops you heard talking about the gangstas. Like it was a piece of garbage you left behind when you were sweeping the men's locker room. You think you could do that?"

She didn't answer. There was a sound at the door and a few of the young cops themselves came in before they headed for a day at court. The receptionist came in, too. She started taking cards and writing names in her book. The cleaning lady found her rag and her feather duster. I took my place on the treadmill.

I had a feeling things were starting to look up. Like it wasn't a waste of time to come to the gym after all. Like things might take a turn for the better for the young cops on the gang case, for Denise, for the cleaning lady, even for my sweet wife, Scott. After all, a husband in shape might not be such a bad thing.

I looked at my old flat feet, realizing it wasn't that hard to see them down there anymore. I got the treadmill up to quite a speed. I walked and walked. Walking on that mill suddenly reminded me of something I hadn't done in a good long time.

It reminded me of walking the beat.

SHAVING WITH OCCAM'S RAZOR

On the way to the morgue I nearly got hit at Wellesley. I was late for forensic class for the third time in five weeks. Not my fault. A heavy day at the office, three parolees facing suspension for suspected drug dealing—I was thinking about work when I ran out of the subway and almost collided with an incoming eastbound bus.

I tore along Yonge, hung a right at Grosvenor, remembered we weren't meeting at the Centre for Forensics like we usually did. Field trip. I zipped back to Yonge, shot down a block and skidded to a halt in front of the coroner's building on Grenville.

So I wasn't in the mood for sarcasm when I was finally buzzed through, managed to locate the lecture hall, opened the door, walked in and found myself standing beside the instructor at the front of a room full of my fellow classmates, all of whom were staring at me as if I were some sort of specimen.

"We're waiting for you, madam. You're late," the instructor announced, dramatically eyeing his watch. I'd never seen the guy before in my life, but already I knew he was a retired cop. The attitude. The Metropolitan Toronto Police seal emblazoned on the face of the watch.

"Not as late as most of the people in this building," I answered.

The class sniggered. The ex-cop looked shocked. Good.

Of course the only seat left was in the front row, right smack in front of him.

"How many times has this man been shot?" he asked me, before my bottom even touched the chair. I suppose he thought he was tricking me. Silly man. I haven't spent the last ten years as a parole officer for nothing. Manipulative people like crooks and cops always ask quick questions hoping to throw people off guard.

I glanced up at the screen behind him. Projected there, in x-ray, was the outline of what appeared to be an adult male. The poor guy was a piece of Swiss cheese—a couple dozen holes in him, fanned across his torso.

"Once. He's been shot only once," I said, settling into the chair and shrugging off my jacket.

"Why, you're right..." The ex-cop's eyes locked into mine for a second. Nice gray eyes. Wary. Wise. The kind that have seen just about everything—or think they have. Right now they were registering surprise again. I smiled. He addressed the rest of the class. "Here we see the typical pattern produced by the impact from a single shotgun shell...."

There was a click from somewhere behind me and a new image flicked onto the screen. It was another adult male body, this time a schematic outline. Beside each part of the body was a tidy list of the types of evidence the forensic scientist looked for: strands of hair, the characteristic indentations produced by a person's teeth, fingerprints...

Beside me and behind me, I heard the frantic scratching of people taking notes. I was the only corrections person in the forensic class. The rest was divided just about fifty-fifty. Half were cops trying to improve their chances for promotion. The other half were mystery writers trying to improve their chances for publication.

I didn't bother taking notes. It was obvious to me what sort of evidence would be looked for—plus we'd been studying it all term. "Forget your pen?" the instructor asked sweetly.

"No, sir," I replied, and I winked.

He blushed. Cops blush all the time. Cry, too. No wonder, considering.

I felt like crying myself when I caught the next slide. It showed the body of a man who couldn't be older than about twenty. He was spread out on a white table. His arms and legs were thin, but still muscular. His thick long auburn hair formed a pool under his head. There was a Y-shaped cut on his chest, one of the beginning steps of an autopsy. In death, his face didn't have any real expression on it, but I couldn't help seeing sorrow there. Inset into the slide was another picture. It showed a small square, sewed together with crooked stitches from two dirty pieces of cloth and attached to what looked like an old shoelace.

"Anybody want to venture a guess as to what this might be?" the instructor asked, using a pointer to lightly tap the square on the screen.

I had an idea, but I kept my mouth shut. I'd had about all the attention I cared to have for one night, thank you.

"Valuables—" I heard one of the cops in the class whisper.

"Yes," the instructor replied. "This is the body of a homeless street person. Tied to his underwear we found—as we often find—a small satchel containing the sum total of his remaining worldly goods."

There was another click, another slide—showing the little squares of cloth separated to reveal the contents—two shining wedding rings, a woman's and a man's.

Seeing this, the writers scribbled faster. The cops didn't bother. There's a million stories in the city morgue, and enough people already who think they can tell them.

"Now, class," the instructor said, "it's your turn. I need a volunteer." Onto the screen came a strange picture. It showed the slender body of what appeared to be an elderly male seated in an easy chair. Over his head was a plastic bag from a well-known supermarket, its logo accidentally looking like a screwed-up human face. The bag was tightened around the man's neck with a rope. One of his arms was bound with the same sort of rope; the other hung limp and free, dangling over the arm of the chair. "I want a volunteer to analyze this scene for me—tell me what happened here—"

Behind me I heard the embarrassed scrunching down into seats of people who didn't want to be called on. I didn't scrunch down. I didn't think the instructor had the nerve to call on me again. Anyway, I didn't care one way or the other. I knew what the slide showed.

He waited. Nobody volunteered. I looked up. Those gray eyes were on me. When I didn't look away, he handed me his pointer. "Tell us—" he said. I thought he seemed pretty sure I wouldn't be able to.

I stood, took the pointer from his hand, turned to face the class. In my best case-presentation voice I said, "Though this is an apparent homicide, what we're looking at here is not really a murder scene—"

I shot the instructor a glance. For the first time, I saw traces of a genuine smile on his mouth.

"Please continue," he said.

I nodded. "First and foremost, there's no sign of struggle—no clothing in disarray, no furniture displaced—" I used the pointer to show a table beside the chair in which the victim sat. It was covered with little knick-knacks—all in a row. "No scratches on the body, no blood...."

"But the man has a rope around his neck—" the instructor interrupted. His voice was challenging, like that of a coach.

"Yes. But it's the same rope that's around his arm. Not just the same kind—the same piece." I slid the pointer along the picture. The rope wrapped around the neck, then seemed to disappear behind the chair, but if you traced carefully, it wasn't hard to figure out that it must loop behind the chair then back around the front—around the man's right wrist. "What this person did," I concluded, "was rig this rope in such a way that when he yanked his arm, it tightened around his neck…."

The instructor was actually looking pleased now. But I wasn't finished. "There are other reasons to believe this is a suicide," I went on. "For starters, homicide is a much rarer occurrence than suicide. So, statistically, the chances of any questionable death being suicide are much higher than it being murder. Also, the victim is an elderly male. Traditionally, males handle being alone much more poorly that females. And though they don't always turn to suicide, of course, they are far more likely to do so than some other segments of society…."

"Thank you, that's enough," he said, taking the pointer from my hand. I couldn't tell whether he was pleased or whether I'd gone too far. Maybe I embarrassed him. At least now he'd get off my back.

"This is an elderly widower who had just learned he had cancer. He killed himself when he got the news. In this case—and in all cases," he said, "it's best to apply a principle referred to as 'Occam's razor'. Occam was a medieval philosopher dedicated to teaching that truth results from the observation of the physical world. He said that the simplest explanation of any phenomenon is almost invariably the truest. When I myself was studying, I was told, 'When you hear hoof beats, think of horses, not zebras.' I can offer no better advice."

With that, he adjourned the lecture. I knew what had to be coming next. He led us down a winding corridor and into a brightly-lit room that sparkled with white enamel, spotless tile, stainless steel. There were drains in the floor.

"The morgue is part of the ministry of the Solicitor General of Ontario," he told us, "and like all government offices, we work business hours. 8:30 to 4:30. No autopsies at night…"

A sigh went around the group that was now huddled around the instructor. Relief from the cops. Disappointment from the writers.

"But here in the autopsy room you can see the atmosphere in which we work—and some of the tools of our trade."

Saws, scalpels, knives, picks, hoses. Microphones and tape recorders. He showed us the video room, where bodies were displayed for next of kin too squeamish to look directly at their loved ones. Scales for weighing dead livers and hearts, jars of organs ready for analysis when "office hours" resumed. A room for isolating bodies infested with insects—whose lifespan, he helpfully pointed out—gave a good clue as to the time of death.

"There is a cycle of death that follows the seasons year after year," he told us. "At New Year's we see cases of people who've died accidentally because of alcohol—choking while asleep, for example. Late winter—early spring, we get people who've gone through the ice on their snowmobiles. Summer brings drownings. Autumn—early winter, carbon monoxide poisoning from furnaces and chimneys poorly maintained…"

As he talked, he led us toward two tall steel doors. There could only be one thing behind them, but when he pulled on the handle and slowly opened them, I have to admit I was shocked.

Because of the smell, which was not of putrefaction, which I would not have expected, or of preservative, which I would have expected. No. The huge refrigerator that held the bodies that were awaiting further action let loose a smell exactly like fresh meat.

I gasped and stepped back. He noticed. A look almost of disappointment seemed to cross his face. I took a breath and stepped back up toward where he stood near the door.

At that moment, he reached down, grasped a steel handle and yanked. Out slid a shelf, not inches from my waist.

And on it lay the corpse of a woman my own age. She was tall and thin. Pretty. Her fair skin was just beginning to be wrinkled. Her blond hair was just a tiny bit tinged with gray. She was naked but her body was modestly covered with a sheet. "What happened?" I found myself asking, even though I knew it was a dumb question.

This was the instructor's opportunity for a smart answer. He could have easily got even with me for my own smartness.

Instead, with the greatest gravity, he said, "That's for my people to find out. And we will not fail her by neglecting to do so."

A few of the students filed by and studied the body. Most, however, headed for the door. I was the last to leave, the instructor at my heels as we twisted along the corridors that led back to the reception area. Everybody was gone by the time I got there.

I turned to thank the instructor, to apologize for my rudeness. But before I could speak, there was a commotion at the receptionist's desk. I heard a distraught woman yell, "Where is she? Tell me where she is!"

I turned. And what I saw nearly made me faint.

It was the woman on the slab returned to life, tall, slender, pretty. Her fair skin was just beginning to show wrinkles. Her blond hair just beginning to turn to gray.

I thought it was some sort of sick joke. Some effort to scare or confuse me.

But when I looked at the instructor's face, I saw an expression of such pity that I realized this was no joke.

And besides, he had completely forgotten I was there. He was stepping toward the woman. He reached out his hand and gently touched her shoulder, like it was something he'd done a thousand times before. Cop. Coroner. Bearer of bad tidings.

I stepped aside. But I still didn't know what was happening.

Then, as if he remembered I was still around, he turned. All he said was "Occam's razor."

I was out in the street, narrowly missing getting hit by the westbound Wellesley bus before I finally figured it out.

ON THE JOB

Brianna stood in the shadows of the doorway and watched the digital clock and thermometer visible on the side of the bank up the street. It was 2:20 a.m. It was eight degrees Celsius. Freaking freezing. Sometimes she wished she could move to Florida. Eight degrees in the middle of June!

She pulled her leather jacket a little tighter around her. The zipper was broken, so she couldn't close it. She was wearing a leather skirt tonight. Its hem was about even with the bottom of her panties, so it wasn't much help against the cold either. She wasn't wearing any panty hose under her stiletto heels, so the tattoo on her thigh was visible. It was a picture of a fist holding a sword.

She shifted from foot to foot. She'd been really unlucky tonight. It was Tuesday—not the best night for action under any circumstances, though earlier there had been a lot of people on the streets coming from the movies. Bargain night or something. Having the streets full of bargain hunters hadn't helped her much. Anybody who was too cheap to pay full price for a freaking movie wasn't going to pay what she cost.

It was the cold that was slowing up business. She thanked God that she didn't have a pimp. A girl could get the shit beat out of her on a slow night like tonight.

She glanced at the clock again. 2:24. Out of the corner of her eye, she saw cruiser 5710 go by. Buck and Sol. She remembered nights when those two would let her and some of the other girls get in the cruiser when it was really cold—just sit there for a while. Buck was being a whole lot more careful now, and Brianna didn't blame him.

She heard a car coming down one of the side streets, so she stepped out of the shadows and moved toward the curb. The car went squealing around the corner. Clearly not a customer.

When she saw the van approach, however, something told her she was going to be doing a little work. It was a nice car, fairly new, well-kept. She breathed a sigh of relief. It was amazing what you could tell about a person just from the way they kept their car. Lots of times a guy with a dirty car was a real slob—a really smelly customer. Whereas a guy who washed his car once in a while probably washed his dick.

She moved a little closer to the street. The driver of the van slowed when he caught sight of her. He turned the corner of the side street and parked halfway down the block. Nonchalantly, Brianna turned and made her way toward the parked van.

He wasn't bad looking. In his twenties. Not too big. He was wearing what looked like a fairly clean tee-shirt. Brianna could see all this when he opened the passenger door, but she saw it not from the overhead light, which he'd switched off, but from the light from a streetlight a little down the way.

He could see her, too, and apparently, he didn't mind what he saw. He motioned for her to come closer.

Standing on the curb, she leaned across the seat, letting her jacket fall open to reveal all that she wore under it—a black bra. She had a tattoo on her breast, too, but he wasn't going to see that just yet.

She knew the first rule, which was: don't get in the car before you negotiate the price.

"Half and half?" the guy said.

"Two fifty," Brianna replied.

"Two-fifty? Are you crazy?" the guy answered. "I can get it for one seventy-five down the street—"

"So go down the street—" Brianna shot at him. It was all an act, really, and it tired her out. There was no real bargaining on the Track, though she saw plenty of guys going from one hooker to another as though they wanted to get a good price. What they wanted was the opportunity to talk to girls. It was pathetic, but without pathetic Johns, where would she be?

"No—wait—" the guy said. He reached in his jeans pocket and took out his wallet. He pulled out a pile of twenties and lay them on the dashboard, anchoring them with a book. It scared Brianna a little when she noticed the book was the Bible, but she couldn't afford to be fussy. She was freezing and she hadn't turned one trick yet that night.

She hopped up onto the seat of the van.

"Down by the beach?" the man asked.

"Yeah, if you'll drive me back here—"

"Sure," the man replied, and they took off, headed east across town.

Within minutes they were in the Beaches—one of the most beautiful parts of town. The streets were lined with lovely old houses and led down to the lake where there was a wide grassy area, then a boardwalk, then the beach itself.

Even on a weekday, in summer the beach was jammed, and on weekends, the area was a zoo, but now it was practically deserted, except for a car parked here or there. Brianna knew what was going on in at least some of those cars, and it really made her laugh. If some of these middle-management types got a clue about what was going on right outside the door of their fine houses, they'd freak.

Her John pulled up at the end of one street, facing the lake. The minute he stopped, Brianna headed for the back of the van. Even on a slow night, her good work habits prevailed. The second rule of the business was the same as for any business: time is money; don't waste it.

The John had his clothes off in no time. Sometimes they asked her to undress them, which she charged for if she could get away with it. Mostly old guys liked shit like that. This one was all business. Down on his back in no time.

When she reached to take off her jacket, though, he stopped her.

"Leave it on—" he commanded. "It makes you look like a boy...."

Brianna smiled. She knew what this one wanted. She started to talk to him, keeping her voice low, making the most of its masculine gruffness.

"You'd like a boy to lick you?" she breathed.

"No—" the guy answered. But he was starting to breathe in the rhythm that to Brianna was dollars and cents.

As she spoke, she stroked him. She was glad he was young. The young ones got it up so fast. "You'd like a girl to lick you?"

"Of course," he sighed.

"Or a boy?"

He didn't answer. She made her voice sound as masculine as she could. He was breathing really heavy now, and she knew it just wasn't going to take long.

"Let's pretend a nice, pretty boy has your dick in his mouth, okay?" she growled, and she began to slide down his lean body, making sure the leather of her jacket touched his skin every inch of the way from his throat to his member that actually jumped up toward her mouth when she reached it.

Third rule of the business: no business without candy. She never trusted the Johns to provide. She reached in her pocket and pulled out a safe, ripped open the package and slid it on the guy. He was an experienced trick. He didn't express any surprise at this. He seemed incapable of expressing anything, breathing as hard as he still was.

She let the leather rub against his balls as she sucked him. He was starting to whisper a name. She closed her ears. She didn't want to know anything personal about any John. All she wanted to know was how close he was to coming because if he came too soon, half of that pile of twenties might go right back into his wallet.

"Take it off," she heard him sigh. "Please take it off—"

She knelt up, removed her jacket and her bra. It was dark in the back of the van, but there was enough light for him to make out a dark spot on her small breast.

"What the hell is that?" he asked.

"Nothing," she answered. "Just a little tattoo."

"It's ugly. Why do people get tattoos?"

"You want to talk or you want to screw?" she said. She wasn't in this for the chit-chat.

"Make me want to screw," he said, and she was sorry about the damn tattoo because now she'd have to start all over again.

Not that it took long. He was hot. He was hungry. He was up in no time. She grabbed hold of him and stuck it in. He went off like a firecracker. Happy Victoria Day!

Before he even stopped heaving, she had her clothes back on.

"So, you going to drive me back to the Track?" she asked, as they both climbed up to the front of the van.

"Yeah, sure, honey," he said. His voice was different now. She'd noticed that lots of times. Before they came, men always sounded a little sucky: breathless and begging. The stupid assholes.

After they came, they always sounded bored and in a hurry. Which was fine, because that was how she felt, too.

He looked at his wrist. "Shit," he said, "my watch fell off. Go back there and get it for me while I start the car, will you, honey?"

Not wanting to waste any more time, she complied. She felt around on the old blanket, but she couldn't find the damn thing.

"It's not back there," she said, as the John turned onto Queen Street, a couple of blocks from the lake.

"Look, honey," he said, appearing not to care about the watch. "I've been thinking. It's kind of far for me to go back downtown right now. I'll let you out here and you can take the street car back, okay?"

"You son of a bitch…"

"Don't argue with me honey or you'll get your face smashed, understand?"

He pulled up hard against the curb, reached across her and threw open the door. He grabbed the pile of bills and shoved them in her hand. "Get out—"

She did. She knew better than to argue. Fourth rule of the business: never take anyone up on an offer to smash your face.

She gave the asshole the finger as he squealed away, leaving her standing on a corner that wasn't even a damn streetcar stop. She walked a block, looking in the windows of the pretty stores on Queen trying to see a clock. When she finally caught sight of one, she saw that it was 3:05.

It was even colder down here by the lake than it had been further up town, and she hoped she didn't have to wait forever for a street car.

She didn't. Within minutes, she saw one go by her in the wrong direction, which meant it would soon loop around and come back toward downtown. She reached into her pocket for a token and found one. She hopped onto the car when it came. It was deserted—only her and the driver. She went to the very back of the car. Some drivers liked to talk. They were very nice men. She really didn't know what to say to men like that, so she got right out of their way.

She felt a little sleepy. She didn't want to give into it, though. Late as it was and even though it was Tuesday, there was at least a slight possibility that she could turn one more trick.

Thinking about it, she reached into her jacket pocket for the twenties, thinking to put them into her skirt pocket, which was a little safer.

At first she just stared at the bills, unable to understand what had happened. Then she remembered the bastard's lost watch. That would explain it. That would explain why she was holding one twenty and a fistful of fives.

She wanted to cry, but that was something she had trained herself never to do. Instead, she thought about what she would do to the guy if she ever saw him on the Track again. She'd make sure nobody would touch the stupid bastard.

Sure, Brianna, sure you will. Most girls had pimps. Most girls would have to deal with the guy even if Brianna told them what he'd done to her. Most girls would rather risk being ripped off by a bad trick that being hit hard by a bad pimp for refusing a date.

She sat back and stared out at the city as the street car made its slow way west. She remembered a nursery rhyme she'd loved when she was a kid, when her grandmother used to read things to her before she went to sleep. The words still rang in her ears sometimes. She wasn't sure she remembered them exactly right after all these years, but they went something like, "Turn, Dick Whittington, turn again, Whittington. The streets of London are paved with gold."

She thought about that. About the streets being paved with gold. What a laugh! What a fucking laugh…

WATER LIKE A STONE

There are some people to whom it's almost impossible to say no, and my wife, Queenie is one of them.

It was the Sunday before Christmas. Outside the window of our apartment, snow fell softly into the fading afternoon light. Already the trees in the river valley were burdened with white, and the Don was frozen solid.

"Not much in the newspaper today," I said.

Queenie nodded, "Guess not."

She took a sip of sherry. Well, not real sherry. Neither of us drinks anymore. What passes for sherry in our home is a distilled juice of yellow apple and white grape, steeped with clove, cinnamon and essence of fig—our wassail.

"Except it looks like somebody got murdered down the street…."

Though the sight of Queenie reading by the light of our fireplace was one of the chief delights of my winter evenings, I didn't look up.

"Yep," she said, "it looks real bad."

I turned a page of the book review section of the *Sunday Daily World*. There was a lengthy piece on Christmas reading. Glossy coffee-table items. A few biographies of prominent Canadian figures. I didn't see any judges among them.

"Blood all over the place." Queenie shook her head, whether in sorrow or disgust, I couldn't tell, glancing up at her for only an instant.

"Some people have everything," she said, "and then they throw it all away."

I knew by the tone of Queenie's voice that she was about to ask me to do something. Something I'd clearly told her I was not about to do again—ever. I gave the book review section a little shake, so that the paper would rustle and she'd get my point, which was: *I'm reading and I'm not interested in solving any more murder mysteries.*

Putting her section of the paper aside, Queenie stood up. For a moment, she gazed through the window where the fat flakes danced in the white air. She moved to the stereo and put on a disc. The sweet sound of a choir filled the room, singing an old favorite of ours, *In the Bleak Mid-winter.*

The words of Christina Rossetti distracted me from the book reviews and I put the paper down.

> *In the bleak mid-winter*
> *Frosty wind made moan.*
> *Earth stood hard as iron,*
> *Water like a stone…*

Queenie picked up her section of the paper but didn't resume her seat by the fire. Instead she came and sat beside me. I reached out to touch her hand. Truth was, I'd do anything for her. Even if I'd sworn not to.

"So," I said, giving her hand a gentle squeeze, "who's this poor unfortunate who threw everything away?"

Knowing my wife as well as I do, I could just tell by the motion of her hand as she slipped it from my fingers and held up the newspaper that she was excited at my interest.

"It's like this," she said. "Just a bit south of here, at the foot of the Scarborough Bluffs on the edge of the lake, there's a place where a lot of houseboats moor for the winter…"

I nodded. "Yes, I know the place."

"Most of the owners of those boats are really rich," Queenie said, "but not everybody. Some people don't have anything *except* the boats. Those are the ones that live down there all year long, no matter how cold it gets. I guess they put all their money into getting one—you know, sort of a pearl-of-great-price thing. Sell all you have…"

"Yes…" Despite the fact that I was now retired from the bench, I still had the judge's impatience at a witness who dragged out evidence by extrapolating on what it all meant philosophically. "So…"

Queenie smiled. "So, Your Honor, I guess you want to hear more after all."

"Keep it brief and to the point."

She leaned over and kissed me on the cheek. "Sure."

I put down the newspaper and gave her my full attention.

"Last night the cops got a 911 call from a distraught guy. He said he came home from Christmas shopping at Eglinton Square just a few blocks from here."

"What time of day?"

Without consulting the paper, Queenie supplied the details. "He said he left the mall at about 4 p.m. He drove south on Pharmacy to Kingston Road, then over to Brimley and down that road that winds to the lakeshore where the boats are…"

"They mentioned his exact route in the paper?" I asked. "Doesn't that seem unusual?"

"No," Queenie answered, "because he told the police he was trying to figure out the exact time he got to the houseboat."

"Yesterday was the last Saturday before Christmas— probably the busiest shopping day of the year," I observed.

"Busiest except for the Feast of Stephen," Queenie said, "Boxing Day, the 26th, when all the sales are."

"Yes. Anyway, that trip would usually take, what, about fifteen minutes? So if he left at 4 p.m., would it still be daylight when he got to the boat?"

Queenie reached across me and grabbed yet another section of the *World*. "Yesterday, Dec. 22, was the solstice, the shortest day. And the sun set…" she ran her finger along a column of figures, "at exactly 4:43 p.m. That means that if the guy left at 4 p.m., he would hardly have any time at all to see anything outside."

"What did he claim to see?" I asked her.

"The victim was lying dead just inside the door. The windows were all fogged up, except for a little scraped patch near where somebody, probably the victim, must have stood to look out. There were footprints in blood all around the houseboat."

I thought about the scene for a minute. As far as evidence went, it was pretty much the ultimate cliché. "And the footprints led to a smoking gun in the hands of a butler?"

"Okay, forget it. I got better things to do with my time…." She stood abruptly, sending the pages of the paper sliding to the floor.

I reached out and pulled her back down beside me. For a few seconds, she glared at me, but I could see the soft light in her eyes. I brushed her lips with my finger. "Lose the frown and keep talking," I told her. "For starters, tell me about this 'guy'."

"It doesn't say too much about him except that he is a 'well-known area retailer', but I sort of recognize the name. I think he's the man that runs that antique shop on Queen Street that sells old letters and manuscripts."

I thought about that for a moment. I'd been in the store once or twice. It was dusty and smelled vaguely of pipe tobacco and oranges. Not unpleasant, but not to everyone's taste. "I don't know how many customers he gets," I told Queenie. "His prices are high and most of what he sells is pretty arcane."

"What?"

"Rare autographs of obscure people…"

"Yeah. But worth a mint to collectors, I guess."

"I wonder if the police think robbery was a motive," I said.

I expected Queenie to consult the paper again, even, perhaps to quote me a phrase or two from whatever the police had said, not that they usually said much on the scene of a crime or at such an early stage in the investigation.

"All the police say is that the victim was the guy's wife and that she died from stab wounds."

"Stabbed with…?"

"That's the thing," Queenie said. "The reporter found out that there wasn't any weapon left at the scene. Anyway—" She took a slow sip of her drink and eyed me over the rim of the glass.

"Anyway, I'm the one who's supposed to figure this out?"

She smiled.

"I don't suppose you expect me to get on my parka and go down there and look around?"

She seemed genuinely surprised at this suggestion. I was surprised at her surprise. What exactly *did* she want?

"A long time ago," she said, "when you were helping me to read some of the books you like so much, we read a story about that guy who solved mysteries just sitting in a chair."

I had to ponder that one for a moment before I figured out what she meant. "Mycroft Holmes?" I finally said. "Sherlock's brother?"

"Yeah. That's the one."

"So you want me to solve this murder the way Mycroft would?"

Queenie nodded.

I stood up and stretched, gazing out at the gathering darkness and the thickening snow.

When I turned back toward the room, Queenie was looking up at me with an irresistible air of expectation.

"Okay," I said. "A man goes Christmas shopping and returns at dusk. He finds bloody footprints and a wife stabbed. He calls the police. They arrive and find the scene as he described it, but there's no weapon. Also, no motive is immediately apparent, though robbery is a possibility since the man has access to valuable documents and is widely known as a person likely to possess such things."

"Right."

"The man and the victim live in a houseboat. All year long?"

"Yes," Queenie answered. I neglected to ask her how she knew this.

"So the two of them live in a confined space. It's Christmas, a difficult time of the year, especially if money is tight because you run a shop with a very limited clientele and what you sell isn't exactly giftware."

"Yeah."

I kept silent for a moment, considering various possibilities. "Okay," I said, "let's say you're a thief. You live in the neighborhood either of the store or of the houseboats or both."

"And…"

"Both of those places—Queen Street where the store is and the Scarborough Bluffs where the boats are—both of those places are mixed neighborhoods, aren't they?"

"Mixed? You mean rich people and people who aren't rich live there together?"

"Yes. But it's a little more complicated than that. As you yourself pointed out, in some neighborhoods in the city, people who are genuinely rich and people who only appear to be rich live side by side."

"Yeah. So?"

"So there's tension—economic conflict, of course. But also the conflict of keeping up appearances."

"Well," Queenie said, "that could sure cause somebody to want to rob somebody else."

"True. But the need to save face leads to other problems as well."

"Like what?"

Queenie was a person who'd risen from a life on the streets to a position of prominence in our community as a tireless defender and servant of the poor, but she had as much pretension as a cabbage. Which was one of a million things I loved about her. I, however, had often been accused of having a high idea of myself. I knew a lot about saving face.

"It takes money to pretend you have money," I answered. "That means there could be arguments between a husband and wife if they disagreed about how their limited funds should be spent."

"All show and no go..." Queenie commented. She loved the pithy sayings of the street people she served.

"Something like that."

"So you don't think this was a robbery?"

"Queenie," I said, coming back to sit beside her, "the fact that no weapon was found means nothing. If the killer was a robber, he might have fled, taking the weapon with him. He might have tossed it."

"The lake was frozen. Even down by the boats. We saw it ourselves the other day. And it's been real cold ever since."

"He didn't need to toss it in water. He could have tossed it into a trash can, into the woods, even onto the road. There's so much slush from the ice and the salt…."

"Or the weapon could be something else," she said quietly.

"Something else?"

She picked up the paper and studied the photo. I leaned over and studied it, too. It was grainy. You could see the body and beside where it lay, you could see what looked like a little pile of ice, as though it had been chipped away from a window—or a path.

"If the killer was a robber," Queenie said, "he picked a stupid time."

"Broad daylight on a Saturday afternoon."

She shook her head. "It doesn't make sense. If the robber thought the couple had money or something else valuable and kept it in the boat, why wouldn't he come at a time when nobody was home? He could see that a person was there if it was broad daylight, don't you think?"

"There's another thing," Queenie said. "This guy, he didn't have anybody working with him in the store, did he?"

"I can't say. I was only there two or three times. Maybe he hired somebody for Christmas."

"That's just it," Queenie said. "The middle of the last Saturday before Christmas is a dumb time for a store to be left unattended by a 'well-known area retailer'!" She wrinkled her face in a gesture of disbelieving contempt.

Our fireside "investigation" ground to a halt. On the stereo, one disc ended and another fell into place. Queenie seemed to have an endless supply of carol renditions. The choir was replaced by a smooth-voiced tenor crooning *Silent Night*. Outside our window, it had suddenly become night, all traces of snow erased by the warm reflection of our home in the depths of the cold window glass.

I thought about that little pile of chipped ice beside the body.

And then I understood.

I had no idea what had really happened to the manuscript merchant's wife.

But I knew what Queenie thought had happened. And I knew why she cared so much.

"They sold everything they owned for the pearl of great price—that boat," I said, keeping my eyes on the fire. "Maybe they were both excited by the idea, at least at first. They took ownership of the boat in the spring when the trees on the bluffs were just beginning to come back to life after a long winter of being covered with ice—the frozen mists off the lake. The two of them worked together to set up their new home. It didn't matter that that was all they had because they loved it. As spring turned to summer, the birds returned. The white gulls soared in freedom over the water. The Canada geese spread their wide returning vees over the beaches.

"It wasn't hard in summer to look like you had as much money as anybody else, because who down by the bluffs dresses in anything but deck clothes in the summer? Besides, summer is the time a retailer is most likely to sell arcane wares to tourists on a street like Queen East."

Queenie said nothing. I took a sip from my glass and went on.

"But when autumn comes, things begin to change. A person—a couple—begins to need to spend most of their time inside. No more barbecues on the deck. Fewer walks along the beach. If you entertain often, as the rich do, you entertain at good restaurants. Or better, at your private club. If you accept an invitation, you also accept the obligation to reciprocate.

"It becomes harder and harder to hide the fact that the money is running out."

I looked around our own home. The marble fireplace with its brass accoutrements, the mahogany bookcases, the paintings… We were blessed in that our finances were secure. But that had not always been the case. Not by a long shot. So both Queenie and I understood what it meant to be poor. The additional burden of having to pretend otherwise must have proven excruciating.

I continued my narrative, my speculation.

"Tensions mount. Ironically, the poorer the couple becomes, the more time they have to spend together in the cramped confines of their boat. Under such circumstances, many unpleasant things become clear, such as, for example, the inevitable accusation…"

"This was all your big idea…" Queenie offered.

I smiled despite the grimness of the tale. "Right. Sooner or later, the husband or the wife comes to the conclusion that all of their troubles result from some decision, some desire, on the part of the other."

"And then there's a fight."

"A man comes home when he should be working. Or a woman is doing things like scraping ice instead of looking for a job," I said. "Whatever the words exchanged, there's an escalation."

"And there's a weapon. A kitchen knife or something?" Queenie asked.

"No." I pointed to the photo. I could see understanding dawn on her face.

"Water like a stone..."

"He picks up a heavy shard of ice. The lake has been frozen solid for a long time. He stabs her. Again and again. Then he goes into the kitchen and washes the weapon down the sink."

The horror of the idea penetrated the peace of the afternoon and stunned us into a silence interrupted only by a sudden fall of embers in the fireplace.

"But you knew that, Queenie."

"What? I didn't know about that ice part."

"No. But you figured out that he was the one who killed her and you figured out why."

She didn't look at me. "How do you know that?" she asked softly.

"The pearl of great price? The fact that somebody 'threw everything away'..."

She nodded.

I took her hand and held it close to my chest. "Queenie," I asked, "why did you put me through my paces? Did you need to prove I still have what it takes?"

Now she did look at me. I could see the love in her eyes, "You'll always have what it takes, Your Honor," she said, "but..."

"But what?"

"But maybe I won't always have what it takes. I'm not young anymore, or brilliant or..."

"Queenie," I said, "what we have here—our home— it's not based on a lie or a wish we can't fulfill or a drama we have to act out. Our home is based on our love."

"But anybody can have a disagreement."

"Of course."

"And anybody can have a fight."

"Right again."

"But—" She lifted our entwined hands, turned them over and softly kissed my palm. "But *we* would never…"

I could have answered that we never angered each other in the least. I could have told her that I loved her more than I loved myself. I could have observed that in my long career as a judge I'd come to the conclusion that domestic violence is not merely the result of a sudden change of fortune.

But all I needed to say, did say was, "No."

GIFTS

Sammy stuck out his hand as if he expected me to shake it. I didn't do a double take or anything like that. I've been a lawyer now for nearly twenty years, and I'm as good at keeping emotion out of my face as a cop, a poker player or a nun. But all the same, Sammy could tell I couldn't bring myself to touch him. I motioned toward one of the wing-chairs in front of my desk. "Please…"

Sammy sat, but he kept his slender body on the edge of the seat, as if he were afraid to soil it somehow.

"Relax," I said, "take it easy. Have some wine…" I reached over to the carafe and poured him a small glass of sweet vermouth.

"*Grazie*," he said softly, then sank back into the chair. He rested his head against the leather. I noticed that his perfectly cut gray hair was thin. In the first memory I have of Sammy, his hair was a black, curly bush. "Your Uncle Sammy looks like Groucho Marx," my grandmother had commented.

There's never been a time when he hadn't been in my life—from the days when he'd told me bedtime stories to the day I'd gotten charges against him dropped (the heaviest charge of his long criminal career: homicide), to today when my frantic mother had called me with the news.

"You want to tell me what happened?" I asked him. I poured myself a drink, then came around and sat on the corner of my desk. It was late afternoon and a ray of sunlight bounced off the glass door of one of my bookcases and spread its reflected flush across the rug, making its pattern look blurry and vague. Sammy looked vague, too, staring at the rug instead of looking me in the eye as we talked.

It was a trick of Sammy's trade to be able to look a person straight in the eye no matter what. It seemed to be failing him now.

"I done precisely as you instructed," he said. "I flew to Boston. I called on your mother. I told her and your father that I'd been sent to give them a special gift for their fortieth anniversary...."

"Nobody stopped you, did they?" I tried not to sound alarmed.

"Nah, Marky. Nobody stopped me. You had that right. I sailed through customs like a ship. Just the way you said I would. Once I reached Logan, I felt sure everything was going to be just fine. I had a redcap handle the baggage. I can't—I mean I couldn't—manage to carry much, as you are aware."

Over the years, Sammy had done a pretty good job of teaching himself to behave and speak like an educated man. He slipped once in a while, but for the most part when he was doing business, he was nearly perfect. His speech patterns had been honed by years of bending the ears of his victims, dazzling them until they stopped paying attention just long enough for Sammy to slide them over the line and into the red.

"At first," he said, "your mother was a little wary. It's understandable. She never forgave me for what happened to your Aunt Mary's pension."

"That's water under the bridge, now, Sammy. Put it behind you. Aunt Mary's dead."

He nodded, but he still didn't look up.

"She took my word for it that I'm straight now, that I'm working for you. She seemed doubtful. Maybe she had some sort of inkling or something. Of course, I didn't tell your mother anything about what was going on here—I mean about why it was a good idea for me to get away for a while." Sammy swallowed, almost as if he were choking something back.

I poured him a bit more vermouth and topped up my own.

"I didn't tell her about somebody killing that guy in my building. I mean there was no reason to tell anybody, was there? I wasn't a suspect, was I, Marky? I had a bullet-proof alibi. You said so yourself."

I reached across and touched Sammy's shoulder. Without warning, my mind flashed back to the first time I'd ever done that. It was while I was still articling—working on bail cases. I'd gone into a police lock-up and he'd been there, awaiting a show-cause. I'd never seen him down and out before. My mother told me he was a businessman. She'd just neglected to mention the business.

Now he reached up and grabbed my fingers in his own. I almost jumped. But I knew just from his touch that it was his good hand that he'd used.

"You aren't a suspect," I told him. "No one can accuse you of killing that man, even though you were the last person to see him alive and the only other tenant of the small apartment building home at the time the police figure he was strangled. Clearly, it would have taken a man with two strong hands."

Now he looked up. His eyes held something I'd never seen there before: terror.

"It's my whole life, Marky," he said in the modulated tones that had calmed many a wealthy widow. "I've wasted my whole life. And now, near the end of it, when I finally have the chance to finish up as a respectable person with a little dignity…Now this."

He held up his hand, the long straight fingers, the firm palm, the supple wrist. "And now, this…"

For a moment, we just sat there in silence. The sun, with the slowness of late spring, shifted to amber, then rust. Then the air in my office seemed to become a soft blue, like the stained-glass wings of angels. I turned on a lamp.

"Your mother and father were really thrilled when I told them about your gift," Sammy resumed. "I tried to be a little suspenseful. I played around with my suitcoat pocket, pretending to be looking for something. Then I pretended to find the envelope. 'What can this be?' I asked, like I never saw it before. 'Seems to be plane tickets to Paris! 'Paris?' your father asked. 'Why in heaven's name would Marky think that his mother and I would want to go to Paris?'"

Despite everything, I had to smile. Sammy mimicked my father exactly. He could imitate anybody's voice. Of course he could.

"'Because,' I told him, 'that's where you go first when you're on your way from Boston to Lourdes.'

"I watched them real careful, Marky, so I could tell you precisely how they looked. Well, I thought your mother was going to cry, she was so surprised and happy. Your dad— well, he's always said he's happy if she is, and maybe it's true. Anyway, it was perfect. I wished you could have been there— the two of them staring at those tickets as if they was tickets to heaven itself." He stopped and took another sip of vermouth.

Sammy Agnello hadn't much worried about going to heaven, it seemed. He had a rap sheet as long as the silk scarf he wore in winter to complement his cashmere coat at those times in his life in which the proceeds of his crimes managed to outlast the time he did for them. Now that he was out on parole, he had to live on whatever I gave him to run errands for me, plus a small disability pension, but he was still an elegant man.

"Yes, your folks looked like a couple of angels," Sammy said. "I should have stopped then. I should of left well enough alone instead of shooting my mouth off." His voice seemed to quaver. In his line of work, a steady voice was as much a necessity as if he'd been a radio announcer.

"I told your parents that you were so excited about all the arrangements that you'd made for them that you'd made a little joke, that you'd said the only thing you were unable to arrange was for them to actually witness a miracle."

Sammy drained his glass. And he slid his hand beneath the lapel of his jacket, as if to hide it from view. I had known him all my life, and I had *never* seen him try to hide his hand, though anybody would have forgiven him for doing so.

"They didn't laugh at the joke, did they, Sammy?" I knew my mother.

"No. We never mentioned it again. All the way over, your mother was so quiet. Almost like she knew something really big was going to happen. Your father was quiet, too, but then he always is. I figured maybe they were praying.

"We get to Lourdes. There's a lot of tourist business, and I was feeling upset by it. It's noisy. Crowded. And my hand started to ache. It hadn't done that in years, but I figured it was because on the way over, I had to help your mother carry her tote bag, and I held it in both hands for a couple of minutes—something I almost never do.

"Anyway, I took them around a little. Your mother sees the crutches, the abandoned wheelchairs, the walkers, the whole thing. It's impressive. I have to admit. But I'm not a religious man, Marky. With my history, how could I be?"

"Plenty of people with your background become very religious later in life," I reminded him.

He shook his head. "Finally," he said, "it's the big event. A Healing prayer session at the shrine. Now your mother's more like herself. Excited. And she wants everything perfect. She's got a new dress. Your father's in that suit he wore when he stood up for me in court the last time. Nice.

"And I'm dressed, too. Only I can hardly do up my shirt because my hand is hurting so bad I had to get your mother to help. And when she did, she accidentally touched my bad hand. I never knew her to touch it before. Nobody ever touched it, really. Anyway, nothing happened. It still hurt.

"We went to the healing. It was scary, Marky. I saw an awful lot of really sick people. I didn't know what to think about it all. A lot of them were children. Bald children. I was watching this one kid while the priest was giving some sort of blessing. She was just kneeling there, looking up. I remember thinking that even bald she was a beautiful little girl.

"All of a sudden, she closes her eyes and she starts to sway, like she's going to faint. Without thinking, I reached out to catch her. And then I saw what was happening. I was reaching out with my bad hand. It hurt like hell. But it didn't look like hell. Not anymore. My fingers were straightened out. I wasn't disabled anymore. Before I could even think about what had happened, I hear your mother shouting, 'It's a miracle. Sammy is cured!' Then everybody is screaming and shoving and touching me…."

Sammy shivered. So did I. I felt sick. I didn't know what to say. There were tears in Sammy's voice, and I think on his face, too, but I couldn't force myself to look.

"Sammy," I said, "they haven't come yet, have they?"

He shook his head again. "No," he said, "but somebody's going to open their trap sooner or later. They'll show up. Cops always do. And what am I going to tell them? That yes, I'm an able-bodied guy now but that I was handicapped at the time that guy got strangled in my building—on my floor even? I'm an innocent man, Marky. You know I am. But I'm also the last person who saw him alive—and aside from the real killer—the only person in the whole world who doesn't have an alibi. And I've got a rap sheet as long as a rope. How are you going to keep me from being hauled in, Marky?"

"You're a fraud artist, Sammy. Not a killer. It's the wrong M.O. You've never gone down for a violent offense before. That's got to count for something."

But not much. We both knew that. For whatever reason, Sammy Agnello was a cured man. But he was also a man with a dead neighbor and a story nobody would believe.

I poured us both another vermouth. I handed back his glass. He reached out and took it in his straight fingers. They trembled a little, the way a baby's legs tremble when he's just learning how to walk.

OLD MAIDS

When I was little, my mother told me that both the Martinelli sisters had had fiancés, but that they went away in the war and never came back. She said someday I would grow up and have a fiancé and that it would be the happiest time of my life. Even now, after more than fifty years, I remember the pictures of all those handsome soldiers that never came back, but what I remember most about the Martinelli sisters was the way they smelled.

My grandmother smelled of spaghetti sauce. Sometimes she'd come into our house on a winter afternoon when the air outside was so fresh and frigid that you wouldn't dream that anything coming in at the door could smell other than cold. I'd run to her and throw my arms around her waist, and even though she'd come all across town on the bus, and taken off her apron, and changed into a smart dress—the way she always did when she visited—she still smelled of warm spaghetti sauce. I figured that was the way married women—especially Italian grandmothers—had to smell.

The Martinelli sisters smelled of *White Gardenia*. You could catch a whiff of it the minute they stepped into the vestibule and shook their fur coats off their shoulders and into my mother's outstretched hands. "The right place for fur is on animals," she always mentioned after they left.

I knew it was *White Gardenia* because I spent part of every Saturday afternoon bothering my cousin who worked in the perfume department of Jenss Brothers on Main Street. She let me smell as many bottles as I needed to until I found out what it was that the Martinellis wore. Of course, our city being as small as it was, my cousin could have just *told* me what perfume they bought. But that would not be right. "Career girls have beauty secrets," she reminded me.

I already had a few beauty secrets. For example, I had a nice collection of used lipsticks—all the same shade. I picked them out of the garbage of my mother's room. When one got worn down flat, she threw it away and replaced it with another. If I was careful, I could use my pinkie to dig a little out of the tube and spread it on my mouth. Of course, I could only do this when my grandmother was babysitting because she always pretended not to notice when my lips became a smeary blur of "Really Red".

Another of my beauty secrets was the fact that, though I was only allowed a capful of bubble bath, I regularly used enough to fill the entire tub with suds. My goal was to make it impossible for me to see even one square inch of my skin beneath the foam. I imagined the Martinellis positively drowning in bubbles of *White Gardenia,* which came in gift sets that my cousin had let me see.

I was allowed half an hour alone to have my bath. Sometimes I would spend nearly the whole time trying to wash all the bubbles out of the tub, but other times, I would pretend to be grown up. In front of the mirror, I practiced talking like the Martinelli sisters, rolling their names on my tongue.

They were not called Betty or Sue or Mary like our neighbors. Nobody ever shouted over a backyard fence to them, "Hey, Betty!" the way my mother did to her housewife friends as they hung bottomless baskets of clothes on the line.

The Martinellis were called Felicia and Antoinette. "Good evening, Felicia," I'd say to myself in the mirror. "And how are you faring these days?" I didn't know what "faring" meant, but I was sure the Martinellis did.

Another reason nobody ever shouted to the Martinellis over the backyard fence was that they didn't have one. Unlike all the married women I knew, they lived in an apartment. "It's a shame," my grandmother said, "all those fine things their mother bought them—dishes, everything. And no house..."

I'd never been to their apartment—to any apartment, actually—but I knew it was on the fifth floor, which meant you could take an elevator to get to it—much more exciting than climbing the concrete steps that led to our bungalow. And downtown, too. Whenever the Martinellis wanted to shop or go to the show—which was often, I was sure—they never had to stand on the corner of Porter and 32nd street and wait forty minutes for a bus. Nor did they have to wait until somebody came home with the car. They took a taxi. "Such a waste," my grandmother said.

I was well aware also that apartments, unlike houses, had balconies where women like the Martinellis could sun themselves in summer. In winter, they went to Florida.

"Where's Florida?" I asked my mother.

"Where people richer than us go," was her answer.

The reason the Martinelli sisters were rich was because they worked at jobs. After she told me how happy she was that she'd married my grandfather and so never had to work in a factory again, my grandmother explained to me that the Martinelli sisters had good clean work. Antoinette was a receptionist at an office. I could just imagine her sitting behind a big typewriter, a switchboard beside her and an interesting parade of people—probably from out of town— marching past her desk every single day.

Felicia, I found out, worked for a dentist. I hated the dentist, so I changed my mirror name to Antoinette.

You could also tell that the Martinellis were rich because of their jewels. On her ears, my mother wore little gold-plated circles, given to her by my father on their anniversary, and my grandmother had pearls left to her by her mother when she died. But the Martinellis wore diamonds and rubies and sapphires and emeralds. Their earrings hung "halfway to their knees," according to my grandmother.

My mother kindly pointed out that the bracelets and necklaces, earrings and pins of the Martinellis were exactly like those worn by the princesses in my books.

"Or career girls," I said.

"What?"

"Nothing."

Of course it goes without saying that the Martinellis were never pregnant or any other kind of fat. Betty and Sue and Mary, when they visited, always giggled and said, "I shouldn't...." when they reached for a second piece of cake or another slice of pie. I never saw the Martinelli sisters take anything but coffee—milk, no sugar. My mother said they were so skinny they'd disappear if they turned sideways. "Like a long drink of water," my grandmother agreed, popping a cookie into her mouth.

Cotton dresses, wool sweaters, nylon blouses that sometimes turned yellow and had to be thrown away—these were the things married women like my mother wore. Or maternity clothes.

Once, when they came to our house before going out for New Year's Eve with men they called, "our beaus," the Martinelli sisters wore strapless gowns of pale satin with wide overskirts ruffled in pleated organdy. They had mink stoles on. Felicia's was black. Antoinette's was the color of champagne. I had never seen champagne, but my cousin had told me all about it.

"How much does a mink stole cost?" I asked my mother the next day.

"The right place for fur is on animals," she replied.

I don't know when it was that I began to realize that what made the Martinellis so different was the fact that they weren't married. Besides being saved from working in a factory and having gold circle earrings and babies, I hadn't yet figured out why women got married, though I was well aware that you needed men for romance.

"This will capture the heart of that special someone," my cousin told me as she squirted behind my ears with the *White Gardenia* tester one Saturday.

"Why do people get married?" I asked her.

"You'll find out," she teased.

"How come the Martinelli sisters never got married?" I asked my mother one day.

For a while, she kept pounding the bread dough she was kneading, as though thinking about my question good and hard. Finally, she answered.

"Felicia and Antoinette are the prettiest girls in our crowd. Always were. They lost their fiancés in the war. Lots of girls did. But they had many other chances to get married—"

"Lots of beaus?"

My mother smiled. "Lots and lots…"

"So how come they never did? Get married, I mean."

She gave the dough a good hard punch. It popped out from under her fist, and she punched it again. "The truth is," she said, "they never found a man who could treat them as well as they treat themselves…."

She picked up the hunk of dough and slammed it back down. "Now," she said, "they're nothing but a couple of old maids."

I thought about that for a pretty long time. What was it like to go to Florida? No boots. No leggings. No helping my father shovel the front walk.

What would it feel like to have a string of emeralds around your neck?

What would it be like to meet exciting people all day long, then come home, take an elevator up to your apartment, sit on the balcony with a coffee, then call a cab and go to the show?

That night, while I still had time before my mother would knock on the bathroom door and shout, "What *are* you doing in there?" I imagined how my own bathroom would be. There would be a shelf beneath the mirror, a nice long shelf. On it would be ranged the complete *White Gardenia* line: perfume, cologne, toilet water. A big bottle of bubble bath. A round box of powder with a thick white puff with a satin circle on the back that had the letters WG written on it in silver.

The next day, my grandmother came to visit. She sat down at the kitchen table with a nice cup of tea and a few cookies. "Gramma," I asked her, "what happens if a person never gets married?"

"Oh, honey," she said, "don't worry. You'll get married. You're pretty as a kitten."

"No, I mean, what if a person doesn't *want* to get married?"

She reached out and pulled me close to her. She smelled of roasted peppers with a touch of garlic. "Well," she said, "you'll end up an old maid. Now you don't want that, do you?"

"No, Gramma," I said.

But I lied.

THE BENCH RESTS

He'd only come to the courthouse to bring his wife her lunch.

Which had been confiscated at Security, of course.

He should have foreseen that. He checked the impulse to shake his head in self-disgust. Yet again, he'd neglected to weigh the new against the old, the probable against the dead certain.

Walking slowly down the long, slippery hallway that led toward the up escalator, he tried to concentrate. What exactly had his wife told him about lunch time? That her testimony might be finished by then? It had been two or three years, but he still remembered that the schedule of the court was as wily as a bronco. No knowing what time she'd really be done.

He mourned the loss of that confiscated lunch, though. He could still make a pretty mean sandwich. He'd even remembered not to include anything that smelled strong. At the last minute, he'd added a nice apple. He hoped that the required noise of crunching wouldn't embarrass his wife if she had to eat in the company of strangers.

Suddenly an old memory flitted through his brain. He was seated on the bench. The court clerk in her smart black robe was directly in front of him, down a level, so that he was looking at the top of her head. He could see that she was pretending to annotate the day's docket. But what she was really doing was silently unwrapping a chocolate bar. The smell of it wafted up to his nostrils. He could stop the proceedings and get her to surrender it....

"Judge Marshall! Come for a little visit? It's so nice to see you."

The voice cut through his daydream like a shiv. He turned and almost banged into a young lawyer with an armful of files. It surprised the old judge to see cardboard folders, pieces of paper sticking out of them willy-nilly in a messy display of mismanaged paperwork. He thought they'd have done away with all that paper by now—put the records on the internet or something.

"You've got yourself quite a pile of documents there," he said to the young man in order to stall for time to remember his name.

"Merkovitch," the lawyer said, as if he knew what the judge was thinking. "I'm Dalton Merkovitch. I worked with you on the Blane case—for three years, actually."

The judge nodded as if he recalled the whole thing. All he really remembered was that Blane was a loser who had got what was coming to him for having killed his best friend in a fit of rage. He glanced at Merkovitch. Prosecution or Defense? He tried a fishing tactic. "Well," he said, "I guess our man's done a bit of time since you and I laid eyes on each other, eh?"

Merkovitch nodded, smiled.

Prosecution, the old judge decided. He nodded and smiled, too.

Squinting just enough to make out the number over the nearby courtroom door, but not enough to make Merkovitch pity him, he gave the door a good push and let himself into the courtroom.

It still smelled the same. The heat of the old, cranky boiler system. The sweat of fear. The mustiness of papers long trapped in boxes and drawers. The hint of camphor from the mothballs that kept the legal robes from being eaten.

It sounded the same, too. Right down to the audible breathing of the entranced spectators, shifting in their hard wooden pews. Some of them were mere gawkers, but not all. It had long simultaneously amused and appalled Judge Marshall that spectators in murder cases always sat in two distinct groups. Family and friends of the victim. Family and friends of the accused. Like witnesses at a wedding of the damned.

"Judge Marshall—a pleasure! Come in!" This in a hushed whisper from the guard at the door, who wasn't supposed to say anything—just usher people in. The judge raised his hand in a small, silent salute. The courthouse was full of well-meaning lackeys like the doorman. There was no way in the world he was going to remember the name of any of them.

He tried to slide soundlessly onto a bench at the back. No such luck. The little metal pull on the zipper of his jacket scraped along the wooden seat. The sound reached the ears of the sitting judge, who turned her eyes on him for just a second, enough to embarrass Judge Marshall into sinking down onto the seat in a slouch.

But in a minute, he decided that the snooty-looking lady judge hadn't recognized him and wasn't likely to glance his way again. He sat up straighter and took the liberty of having a good look around.

The first thing he saw was that he was sitting with the family of the accused. The man in the prisoner's box was surrounded by glass walls, guarded by two strong-looking young officers, and possibly even shackled to the floor, though nobody but the guards would know that. Yet it wasn't hard to see that the offender was a handsome boy with a distinctive look that Judge Marshall thought marked him as a southern European—Spanish or Italian. He'd taken as many ethnic sensitivity training workshops as the next judge, so he knew that you weren't supposed to even think about such things.

But a lifetime in the law, first as a family lawyer, then in criminal law, then as a prosecutor and finally as a judge, had taught him to take note of everything. And he noticed that the man in the box looked exactly like the people sitting in the three spectator rows ahead of him. There must be thirty of them.

Wait a minute! *Roma*, that's what they looked like.

He was puzzling over whether that might mean anything, trying to remember things he'd lately read about the prejudice against that particular group the way he'd once read about the history of particular groups, when he felt that someone was studying him as intently as he'd been studying his neighbors.

Dismissing ridiculous old ideas about the evil eye, he looked up.

And he saw his wife glaring at him right from the witness stand!

He'd forgotten that he'd promised her that he wouldn't remain in the courtroom during any portion of her testimony. He had very little idea of what she intended to say. They'd agreed to keep it that way. Well, it was too late now. He shrugged his shoulders.

But she didn't see the gesture. Her eyes were back on the prosecuting attorney as he shuffled his papers, stalled for effect, spoke.

"One final thing, Mrs. Marshall. When you entered your garage on the evening in question, were you alone?"

"Yes. My husband always goes grocery shopping with me. But he lags behind. Talking to people in the elevator and things like that. I just go ahead and wait for him in the car."

"Thank you." The lawyer smiled slightly, then dipped his head in the direction of the defense table, as if he were turning over his witness for cross-examination with the greatest of confidence.

The defense rose. Yet another young man. They all seemed like children, even the lady judge. Even the grandmothers of the accused were younger than old Judge Marshall and his wife. He almost let out a sigh, but he caught himself in time.

"You told the court you were headed out to do your grocery shopping the night my client was arrested, did you not?" the defense began. He had a grating sort of voice, the kind Judge Marshall knew his wife hated.

"Yes." She closed her lips tight after that one word.

"And you also stated that you and your husband usually do your grocery shopping together? Isn't that what you told my friend here?" He nodded toward the prosecutor, who did not respond.

"Yes, but…"

Judge Marshall tried hard to avoid eye contact. The reason his wife didn't want him in court while she was testifying was because she felt he'd exercise some sort of undue influence on her. He thought that was batty, but she maintained that after nearly fifty years of marriage, she could tell what he was thinking by the way he was looking at her.

What he was thinking was this: That the night his wife had seen a dark-haired man running through the parking garage beneath their condo, he, himself, had been sick in bed. He knew for certain that he'd stayed home that night because he'd watched the season finale of *The Great Race*. In fact, much as he would have hated to admit it, he'd really not been that sick. He'd just wanted to see who'd win. The show had been half over when his wife had walked out the door. He was sure of it, because the winner hadn't been revealed yet and he remembered feeling relieved that he could watch the most important part of the show without her interrupting him by talking while he was watching, which was a bad habit of hers.

"Mrs. Marshall..." the lawyer said, swaying a little. Judge Marshall wished the man would stand still—wished he could tell him to do so, as he had so often told lawyers in the old days. "Mrs. Marshall, are you sure you allowed yourself to be unaccompanied during those moments in the garage on the evening in question? Don't you think it was rather late to be in an underground garage alone?"

"I beg your pardon?"

His wife's tone was sharp. Judge Marshall knew what that meant. Her toes had been stepped on.

"I'm asking you whether you are sure there were no other witnesses present in the parking garage that late at night."

"You think I'm too old to go out at night?"

An audible gasp spread across the gathered court the way the leak of air from a kid's balloon would spread across the condo party room.

The head of the presiding judge snapped around. "Just answer the question," she warned.

By the look on his wife's face, Judge Marshall knew the exact thought that was going through her head. *Nobody can tell me what I'm too old or not too old to do.*

"Maybe I can rephrase that a little," the lawyer said. He glanced toward the jury, and for the first time, Judge Marshall took a look at the lucky twelve. There was a pretty good mix of male and female, young and old. A witness like his wife was a sure bet with a jury like that. They would believe whatever she said. The old people would identify with her as an equal. The young people would be reminded of their grandmothers—or maybe their ancestors....

"You state that you entered the parking garage at about 8:30 p.m. You state that you saw a young man who fit the description of my client running through the garage at that time. Is that correct?"

"Yes."

The defense attorney grinned. Judge Marshall could only see the lawyer's face because the man had turned around to face his client. The accused himself seemed suddenly frightened. He tried to turn around as if to seek some kind of support from the thirty look-alikes behind him. The lawyer turned back to face Mrs. Marshall. "Madam," he said, "your testimony puts my client in the garage one full hour before the crime was committed, doesn't it?"

Justice Marshall saw the look of shock on his wife's face. "But--?"

The prosecutor rose as if to make an objection.

But even the jury seemed to understand that there was nothing to object to. He sat back down. He frantically searched through the papers in front of him with such energy that Her Honor had to ask him to be quiet.

"I saw him running," Mrs. Marshall stuttered. "It was him—"

For a wild instant, Judge Marshall thought his wife was pointing in his direction, but of course she was really pointing to the prisoner.

"My client doesn't deny being in the garage, Ma'am. You're aware of that fact, are you not?"

"Yes. But—"

"In fact, it is his contention that he left prior to 9 p.m., the time at which the murdered woman made a frantic phone call to her girlfriend."

The defense lawyer paused. Judge Marshall knew the pause was meant to give the jury time to consider what they'd just heard—to come to the only possible conclusion, which was that his wife had just destroyed the Crown's case. In the silence, Judge Marshall could hear all those old familiar sounds again. The breathing of the people in the court, the useless rifling of papers that could prove nothing, the sigh of relief of a killer about to be let off…

And of course Judge Marshall knew it was not the prosecutor who had made a mistake. It was his wife. If the murdered woman had been alive at nine p.m., she would have been alive at the beginning of *The Great Race*. How long did it take to strangle somebody, then to run down seven flights of stairs? About as long as it took to find out who had won the race.

He'd been a judge for a long time. A lot of case law began to reel itself out in his mind. The Crown versus this one and that one.

Would he stand up, like someone out of those old *Perry Mason* shows and set the record straight?

Would he take aside that nice guard who had greeted him at the door and tell him that he needed a word with Her Honor?

Would he send some sort of signal to his wife to alert her to her error and get her to change her testimony?

Thinking hard as he was, he missed what happened next. But he soon figured that either the judge or the prosecutor had called for the lunch recess. Because the jury filed out and then his wife left the stand and made her way toward the table where the prosecutor stood. There was some sort of exchange between the lawyer and his wife, but Judge Marshall couldn't hear anything. The lawyer's back was to him, and his wife was so short that he couldn't even see her face, hidden as it was by the broad shoulders of the prosecutor.

What Judge Marshall had once liked most about sitting on the bench was that he could take all the time in the world to make up his mind about most things. Send a man to jail for life? *I'm giving it some thought*…. Call a mistrial and begin all over again at a cost of a couple hundred thousand dollars? *I'll let you know.*

But of course, he didn't always have that luxury. Sometimes he had to make up his mind in a single instant.

Now seemed such a time.

What he decided was to keep his mouth shut. He hadn't tried to influence a witness in forty years—not since his last day as a practicing lawyer—and he wasn't about to start now.

The accused was led out of the court and his relatives filed out, too. Judge Marshall was the last one of the spectators to leave.

Just as he got outside the door, he heard a familiar whisper. The door guard was standing there. He had a paper bag in his hand.

"Security sent this up to you," the man said proudly—like one who is pleased to offer impeccable service of some sort. "They said you might be needing it."

Mrs. Marshall's lunch!

The Judge took it. He reached out and shook the man's hand. In the old days, he would have said, "Good man," or "Well done." These days such remarks were considered patronizing. "Thanks," he said to the guard. "Thanks a lot."

He took the lunch and walked slowly toward the down escalator. He thought the best thing was just to sit downstairs by the door for a while. For almost the whole of his career in this courthouse, there had been back door, side doors and more than one front door to use as exits, but since 9/11 that had changed.

Now there was only one exit. If his wife decided to go out—or even to come looking for him—sitting by the exit was his best chance of seeing her—or of her seeing him.

But he didn't think that would happen.

He figured that the lawyer would take her back to his office—the Office of the Prosecution in the secure area on the first floor and that together they would somehow try to undo the damage she'd done to the case.

Judge Marshall decided to wait for half an hour. Then, he would go home.

And if she wanted to explain what had happened, how she had made such a terrible mistake, then she could tell him.

Otherwise, he would just keep his own peace.

Concentrating as he was on these thoughts, he jumped when someone was suddenly standing in front of him, blocking the light from the exit's barred window they'd installed right after 9/11.

"It was eight-thirty. You and I have gone grocery shopping every Thursday at 8:30 since we moved into that condo. Plus, I probably would have checked my watch to make sure the store would still be open."

"If we did the same thing every week for years," Judge Marshall said, "why would you need to check your watch? Besides, that store's twenty-four-seven—has been for five years."

"Don't talk to me like I'm Alzheimer's," she said.

That grim possibility had never occurred to the judge, but it did now. He looked at his wife. *Nah*.

She had just made a simple mistake, that was all.

"Everybody's wrong once in a while," he said. "Want some lunch?"

She glanced at the paper bag where he'd placed it on the seat.

"Why don't you sit down for a minute?" He picked up the bag and patted the empty place beside him.

Mrs. Marshall sank into it. She'd always been a small woman. That was one of the things he loved about her. In the old days, he used to call her "my pocket wife" the way he called his favorite book "my pocket criminal code." She seemed smaller than she'd ever been. No, he reminded himself. That was stupid.

"I told that lawyer right from the start that I was in that garage. He looked in all his papers but he can't find where he wrote it down. He thinks I'm the one that made a mistake. He thinks he can still fix things if…

She looked up at him. He could see she was fighting the urge to ask him for help.

"It's a good sandwich," he said. "No onions."

She accepted half the sandwich and took a bite. She chewed carefully, swallowed, shook her head.

"When people do the same thing every week of their lives, how can they make a mistake about what they did?"

Judge Marshall didn't answer. He was thinking about the Blane case, the one that Merko kid had worked on with him. He remembered there had been some sort of time mistake there, too. It wasn't that unusual for several witnesses to an event to give differing times for the same occurrence. One of the things that working in court for fifty years—heck, for fifty minutes—soon taught a person was that eye-witnesses were often the worst kind. And the more eye-witnesses there were, the more conflicting stories might be told.

In the Blane case, Judge Marshall had seen a discrepancy right from the word go. Of course, it wouldn't have been his place to say anything to the witnesses, though he might have held some sort of a hearing with the lawyers if it had become necessary.

But it hadn't been necessary. The erring witness had suddenly remembered that on the night in question, she had been on the way to her sister's birthday party. An easy-to-remember event like that—the jury had believed her. The erroneous testimony had been rescinded. The record had been corrected.

But what did that have to do with his wife?

She was picking at her sandwich as if she had no appetite.

"Something wrong with the sandwich?" he asked.

"No."

"Not fresh enough?"

"What?"

"I used the lettuce we bought last night."

"Last night?"

"Oh, come on," he said with mock impatience. "Now are you going to tell me that you can't remember that we went grocery shopping last night?"

"That's right," she said absently. "It's Friday today. Thank God."

"Thank God?"

"Yes. No matter what happens to me this afternoon, there won't be any court tomorrow."

"Nothing's going to happen to you this afternoon," he said. But it was a sort of lie. Because at the very least, there would be some sort of re-examination, and that would give the prosecutor plenty of time to grill his wife.

"You know," she said, "all the years you worked in court, all the cases you tried—"

"Yes."

"You never talked about them when you came home."

"So?" Was she going to tell him that he should have shared his experiences so that she could have learned how to be a better witness? That didn't make any kind of sense.

"So I got used to thinking that you had this—I don't know—this other life—like some sort of mystery existence or something." She stared into the air in front of her for a minute. Then she smiled. Judge Marshall felt a pang. The smile looked awfully sad. "But the fact is, when you retired, I could figure out that you must have been the same way in court as you were at home...."

"Meaning?"

"Always doing the same thing at the same time. Routines. That's why we always shopped on Thursday. You said routine was important. You said if you do the same thing at the same time as often as you can, you—"

She stopped. Again a look of shock crossed her face. But only for an instant.

"I remember."

"What?"

"I remember it wasn't 8:30 at all. It was 9:30."

Judge Marshall popped the rest of his half of the sandwich into his mouth. In order to avoid saying anything.

"You weren't with me because you were sick. When it got to be almost 8:30, I asked you if you were ready to go and you said you didn't think you could handle it. I told you I'd wait half an hour to see whether you might feel better, and I did wait, but by the time I got my cloth shopping bags together and checked with you to decipher the list you wrote in your terrible handwriting, and found my own keys to the car, it was past 9. I remember that I thought it was great the way you didn't tell me it was too late to go out by myself...."

Judge Marshall laughed.

95

But his wife became agitated again. "How am I going to convince them?"

"Of what?"

"How can I make them believe that this time I know what I'm talking about?"

He could have offered to speak to the prosecutor and offer himself as a witness. He could have told his wife about *The Great Race*, admitted that he'd not been as sick as he'd pretended to be.

He could have quoted those cases he'd thought of up there in the courtroom when he'd realized she was making some kind of fool of herself.

But he didn't.

He hadn't worked in the courts for fifty years without realizing that justice, like every other game in town, is a crap shoot.

Before she'd gotten in this mess, she'd told him to stay out of court when she was on the stand. Because she knew that he could influence her. And even without his legal training, without his having told her year after year what he had been doing all those days in court, she had understood that it wasn't fair for her to use any recollection except her own.

That hadn't changed. She was the witness. Not him.

And she was a cute little old lady. A jury who didn't believe her deserved to be responsible for letting a murderer go free.

If he *was* a murderer.

Judge Marshall reached into the paper bag on his lap.

"Look," he said, "an apple. Let's share it."

"Like Adam and Eve?" his wife said.

"No," he answered. "Like you and me. Every man for himself."

His wife smiled again. A sweet smile. Anybody who took her for a liar deserved to get whatever they had coming.

THE BIKER AND THE BUTTER

"Them damn cons is going to kill me. It says so right here. They're animals—nothing but animals. And now they're going to kill me...."

"Jass, calm down. It's a joke. I'm sure it's only a joke." I took the note from her hand. It smelled of stew. There was a little bit of bright orange carrot stuck to it, and a big spot of grease made some of the words nearly illegible. It was written in pencil on a piece torn out of a brown paper bag. All the letters were capitals.

"Your cooking sucks," it said, "and so do you. You're dead meat. Just like you feed us."

"It's that biker," the cook said. "I should of knowed before coming to cook at a damn halfway house!" Now she was weeping. Big tears were sliding down her face. She was a middle-aged black woman from Jamaica. I'd tasted her cooking. Once she gave me a piece of apple pie. It didn't taste bad, but when I'd got halfway through it, I found a little piece of raw broccoli. Nothing to worry about, but it took my appetite away.

"It's that biker—He's after my ass. He thinks he's smart. He hates blacks. All them white cons do...."

"Jasmine—" I came around from behind my desk in the reception alcove and stood beside her. I felt sorry for her. I felt like putting my hand on her shoulder or patting her on the back. But I didn't touch her. It was a rule of the halfway house that nobody touched anybody else under any circumstances. Touches could so easily be misread. "Jass, I'll take it up with Ms. Fulsome-Bright. I'll tell her you were threatened...."

"Nothing she can do," Jasmine said, still crying, "I still gotta cook for them beasts."

I handed her back the note. "At least Ms. Fulsome-Bright can find out who wrote it."

"I told you, that biker wrote it. Acts so big around here. Well, there's people inside can fix him—"

I stared at her. Was she implying that she *knew* somebody inside? That was against the rules, too.

"He can't read, Jass. And that means he can't write."

She just laughed. "He can read all right. That whole literacy thing's just a scam. Make you think they can't read. You a bigger sucker than Ms. Fulsome-Bright." She laughed and shrugged her shoulders. "Do me a favor and don't tell Fulsome-Bright nothing. If they think I'm poisoning them, maybe I should start." She threw the note in the trash and stomped back to the kitchen. I got the feeling there was going to be a lot of hot jerk coming out of there for some time.

I called it my day job. Running the halfway house office was my only job, of course, but I sometimes needed to feel that a fifty-year-old woman with a university education working as a secretary had to explain herself somehow and that was how.

The days were like my days everywhere. Things to do and people to look after, usually at the same time. The things to do—parole reports, travel passes, petty cash, scheduling community visits so that the parole officers could visit the offenders' families—weren't hard. Looking after people *was* hard. Because I wasn't supposed to be doing it. "You're not a social worker," my boss told me, "not responsible for the inmates in any way, except to hand out transit tokens, check travel passes and sign clients in and out of the house when they leave for work—you got that?"

"Yes," I told her. She was very young and relatively inexperienced. She'd become the director during a government program to give women under thirty the chance to advance their careers without prejudice due to youth. Like most people who are well educated but lack experience, she went by the book. "I'd like you to sign this," she'd told me when she hired me. It was a form stating that she had the right to fire me without warning if I made the mistake of "interfering in the personal life or legal situation" of an offender." I signed.

All of the inmates, I mean the clients, were men coming out of federal prisons. They had become desperate and hardened, not by going to jail, I thought, but by the kind of life that eventually sends you there. I was afraid of them at first. Then, gradually, in various ways, I became afraid for them.

Nonetheless, I kept clear, as they would say.

I would have forgotten about Jass and the note except that an hour later I took a lunch break and walked out onto the wide verandah of the halfway house. Pete Peters, the "biker," was sitting out there, and he was reading *AutoBuy* magazine.

"Hello, Pete," I said pleasantly. I liked Pete. Everybody said he was a biker, and he had the sort of roly-poly look of some of them. I'd heard they stayed fat in order to hide the fact that they had so many muscles. I didn't know whether that was true or not. My university degree is in criminology, and I could tell you about the international organizational structure of motorcycle gangs and the chief crimes for which they are responsible throughout North America, but I wasn't sure about the fat.

I wasn't sure about "colors" either, though I'd seen Pete wear a vest with a patch on it once or twice. One of the other cons had seen him and laughed. "Nothing but a baby biker," the con had sneered. I wasn't sure what he meant.

Pete was studying the magazine with an intensity that was almost impressive. "Any bargains in there?" I asked.

He smiled up at me. He still had most of his teeth. The federal government had a decent dental program for men inside, but it didn't cover what a lot of them really wanted: gold caps. Pete's teeth were all white. Pete was white. About thirty. Not bad looking. His hair was long, but very clean. A wisp of it rose in the breeze that brushed by the porch. It was July. I figured that when Pete's full parole was granted, he'd go back to being a full-time biker. Then his hair wouldn't look so soft and clean. I didn't know whether it was out of boredom or just the pleasure of being alone in the shower for the first time in a long time, but the men at the halfway house were about the cleanest people I ever saw in my life.

Pete pointed to the magazine. "Look at this," he said, "a brand new Caddy for under a hundred grand…"

I came a little closer, leaned over, looked where he was pointing. I saw a picture of a car and a row of figures, but I couldn't get close enough to make out what they were. I would have moved closer, but I didn't want to break the rules by accidentally touching Pete.

I talked to Pete on the porch a few times after that. There wasn't a lot to talk about at first. People who live in halfway houses don't talk about the past or the future as a rule. And their present isn't very exciting. Get up. Fix your own breakfast. Look for work. Come back. Take a shower. Eat a supper cooked by Jass. Go to AA. Watch TV. Play video games. Sign the curfew sheet. Go to Bed. Get up. Fix...

One day, though, something interesting happened to Pete. A man came for him in a limo. I was sitting in the reception alcove marking up the phone bill. Each parole officer had a list of approved phone numbers they could dial and I was matching up the bill with the list. "Accountability," Ms. Fulsome-Bright chirped as she passed my desk.

I was thinking something unsayable about her when the phone rang, making me jump. "Briarwind Correctional Residence," I said.

"Tell Petie to look out the window," came a low, commanding voice.

Of course my first reaction was to look out the window myself. Parked at the curb in front of the swinging Briarwind Correctional Residence sign (painted by inmates still inside) was the longest, lowest, darkest car I'd ever seen. Every window was heavily shaded. I couldn't see anybody in it. Not even the driver. I always thought that was against the law. But whoever was in that limo wasn't worried about a little offense like a window tinted a shade too dark.

"Phone calls to residents while they are present are to be made to the house cell phone only. Would you like the number?"

"Stuff it up there, sister," came the voice. "Just tell Petie to haul his ass out here."

I did. And when Pete came down, I was shocked to see he was dressed in a suit. He looked far more like a businessman than he did a biker. *Maybe all those rumors are wrong....*

Pete smiled at me as he reached for the sign-out log. "Job search," he said. I had standing instructions to accept that as a sign-out excuse at any time during business hours.

Ms. Fulsome-Bright had reminded me that trust is part of rehabilitation. She also reminded me that anybody out of the house after six without a pass would be back in jail within the hour.

So I couldn't question Pete. And anyway, I was alone in the house. Fulsome-Bright was at a community relations meeting and the parole officers were doing institutional visits—fishing for more residents for the house for when the present bunch made full parole and left. "Good luck, Pete," I told him.

"I need it," he said. He sounded like he meant it, but of course it was against the rules for me to ask why.

I never saw the limousine again and whatever the job was, Pete didn't get it.

But the letters started coming for him. It was my job to distribute the mail. By the time the letters for Pete started, I'd forgot about the note threatening to kill the cook. I didn't remember it until I saw the look on Pete's face when he got the first letter. I thought it must be a love letter. And of course, I thought Jass must have been right. Why would an illiterate man be so happy to get a letter?

After that, he got one every week. Though I wasn't supposed to, I read the return address. It was local. And the handwriting was flowing and feminine.

I guess it must have been about a month later when Jass asked me to go to the store for some butter. When the parole officers were in, I often went to the store for things— odds and ends that we'd forgot to include in the weekly order we had delivered from a cut-rate food warehouse. But on that day, there was nobody in the house but Jass and me. To have left her alone there was against the rules. I was explaining that to her when Pete walked by. It was against the rules to send the clients on errands, but not as against the rules as it was to leave Jass alone.

"Pete, can you run over to Sam's and get us a pound of butter?"

Pete nodded. I took the money from petty cash and sent him on his way.

It seemed like a very long time before he came back, and when he did, he just plunked a small white plastic bag on my desk, along with a few coins, and took off upstairs to his room.

I opened the bag. Inside was a foil-wrapped object exactly the size and shape of a pound of butter. On it, in large red letters was written, "Lard."

I snuck out of the house, took it back, got the butter, gave it to Jass and said nothing to Pete.

But the next day, I went to the downtown literacy center. They gave me books written especially for what they called, "disadvantaged low-attention adults with specific reading skill insufficiencies." *Our Trip to the Bank* showed several adults of varied ethnic backgrounds filling out deposit slips and presenting them to the teller....

"Those are for retards," was Pete's simple reaction. It didn't seem to bother him at all that I'd figured out his secret. He didn't even seem to mind my offer to help him learn to read and write. Maybe the fact that it was so forbidden by the rules was in my favor. A biker is an outlaw, after all. But it bothered him greatly to be lumped in with others who couldn't read.

I left the books with him anyway, as the literacy center had suggested. Next day, when I was emptying the office trash, I found that somebody had put the literacy books through the shredder.

But the letters kept coming for Pete, and now I knew that he couldn't read them or answer them. It must be a very persistent lover, I thought, who would keep sending those letters when they weren't getting any response. Of course, one of the other house residents could read the letters for Pete. I was fairly sure that that was how he had got along so far. I figured out, for example, that he had probably dictated the letter to Jass. There was no one else in the house articulate enough to have composed it. But would he let another man read a love letter?

The reason I knew Pete was articulate was that he and I were chatting almost daily now. He told me a little about his motorcycle. And one day, he told me about his daughter. Just what she looked like and how old she was.

I was at my desk at the time, and Pete was standing in front of it. I was at the computer, keying in a rejection letter that Ms. Fulsome-Bright was sending to some poor social sciences student begging for a placement. "I'm sorry to inform you," it began.

But when Pete started talking, I idly began typing not the letter, but his words. "My daughter's name is Julia. She's a sweet kid. Don't look like her old man in the least…."

When I finished, I ran the page off on the printer and handed it to Pete.

"What the hell is this?" he asked.

"It's your words—"

"What do you mean—my words?"

"It's what you said about your daughter. I put it down in writing. See—"

I read it, pointing out each word. Pete seemed amazed.

After that, we worked an hour a day. I used my lunch hour when Fulsome-Bright wasn't around and the parole officers were downstairs in the kitchen eating with the clients.

We made progress. In a week, Pete could write his name, address and the names of everybody in his family, whatever of his family he could remember, that is. In two weeks, he could write a couple of sentences. In three weeks you could send him to the store with a list and he could come back with most of the things on it.

Of course, all this was highly risky, and it would have come to a bad end sooner or later. But never in my wildest imagination did I foresee what would really happen.

The beginning of the fourth week of our working together, Pete Peters was found shot dead in the alley behind the halfway house.

To make a long story short, there were all sorts of investigations. After quite a while, the police figured out it had been a hit from inside. One of those complicated things that involved communication between men still doing time inside and men on the outside who owed them favors. I never did learn what it was that Pete had done that cost him his life.

But I did learn that it was not knowing how to read that killed him. Because the day of the shooting, when everybody else was out in the alley with the police and the media, I went up to Pete's room. I wanted to find the papers we'd worked on—the print-outs of our conversations. I didn't think they'd have a thing to do with what had happened to Pete, and they'd have a great deal to do with my being fired if they were ever found.

It wasn't hard to find them. They were shoved into a hole in the mattress. He'd saved every piece of paper. And of course, he'd saved every "love" letter.

I had no intention of reading the letters, of course. I was just about to put them back in the hole when I noticed something odd. I noticed that each letter had a double envelope. Pulling one letter apart, I saw that the first envelope bore the return address of the prison where Pete had done time. The outside envelope, of course, was the one with the flowery handwriting.

An old trick. A con inside sends a letter to someone outside who then remails it.

I started to read the letter itself. It was brief. All it said was, "We're waiting for the information, Pete. Send it now."

Before I could read another word, I heard footsteps, the light, nervous steps of Fulsome-Bright herself. She was going to demand to know what I was doing. And I was going to have to think fast to find something to tell her.

I shoved Pete's letters back into his mattress and rearranged the blankets as best I could.

I kept the printouts, though. I pushed them into the pocket of my sweater. I managed to get out into the hall before the boss saw which room I was coming from.

"What are you doing up here?" she asked.

"I needed to use the washroom. The one downstairs had a cop in it."

She nodded, motioned toward the stairs. I preceded her down and sat at my desk, pretending to work at the computer.

Later that afternoon, Jass came up from the kitchen. She was crying again. She stood in front of my desk with a small white piece of paper in her hand. She pushed it under my nose. It smelled of stew. There was a bright green piece of pea stuck to it.

"Nobody's all bad, you know that," she said.

"What do you mean?"

"A guy apologizes and the next thing you know, he gets shot...."

"What?"

I looked down at the paper. "Jass, it says, 'I'm sorry....'"

"I found it in the pot, just like that other note. He wrote it. He apologized."

"But it's typed—on a computer!"

"Doesn't matter. I know it's him. They can type and use computers and read and everything. And anyway, I seen you both. I know you was teaching him things. At least he was a man. At least he apologized for threatening to kill me."

I handed her back the torn slip of paper. There wasn't much I could have done for Pete Peters. Even if I could have taught him faster, I doubt he could have read and understood whatever instructions were in that stack of letters. But at least someone would have a forgiving memory of him....

I went back to work. There was a lot of confusion, of course, but right in the middle of it, a cab pulled up and a very young-looking man wearing prison-release denim and carrying a small duffle bag got out of it and started up the walk.

I checked my list. A new resident. Not really due for several hours, but here now. Disoriented. Facing life on the outside after who knew how long inside.

When he saw the cops buzzing around, he looked shocked, then terrified. I felt sorry for him. I left my desk, went out onto the verandah, met him on the walk. I led him up the path toward the house.

Just as we got to the steps of the verandah, I looked up. Fulsome-Bright was looking out the window—right at me. Her expression seemed to warn me that I had just broken the rules and was going to face the consequences.

I looked back at her. I smiled. Silently, I mouthed a greeting. "Stuff it up there, sister," I said.

SAFE WATER

I see at once that I'm the only one. And I know it's going to be even hotter inside than out. The minute Daddy and I step through the door of St. Emmet's Church Hall, I notice the tiny air conditioner groaning with slow inefficiency at the window, the dewy mustache of perspiration marring the shaved perfection of the welcoming chairman. On the long refreshment table covered in white plastic, the various homemade dips have gone liquid inside partially dismantled circles of limp crackers. A lazy fly investigates, loses interest, moves away. In a corner, a few elderly men hover around a refrigerator, fiddling with a drinks dispenser in the center of the door. A circle of wives waits, each with two large plastic glasses in her hands.

"Gave me a minute's pause, young lady," the grinning chairman declares, taking my fingers in a surprisingly strong grip. "Figured one of us had found the fountain of youth. You don't look a day over thirty-five."

"My daughter," Daddy says, his smile the same as always—warm, genuine, unrevealing, "my daughter Teresa."

"The writer," the chairman offers. "We know all about her, now, don't we? Only daughter to show up at the reunion—and no sons."

Daddy's smile widens and I can't tell—never could—whether from pride or embarrassment. "Let me get you a drink, honey," he says. "Beer okay?"

I nod, not really willing to relinquish him to the group around the beer spigot. He's the only person I know in this crowd gathered to celebrate the fiftieth anniversary of their high-school graduation.

111

With his hand on my waist, he leads me toward the fridge. It occurs to me that Daddy has always led me through crowded rooms like this, just the way the heroes in the romance novels I write for a living lead the heroines. I try to remember whether the men I'm seeing at the moment do that.

"Pete Minelli—the brain! Pete!" A hearty voice interrupts my thoughts as a small, round, bald man grabs my father's hand and begins to pump it as though that were the only way to get the words to flow from Daddy's mouth.

"Bobby, isn't it?" Daddy asks, his smile gracious. "Bobby Malloy. It's been a long time, hasn't it?"

But Bobby doesn't answer. "Hey, hon," he cries to a large woman in a fuchsia cotton dress that matches exactly her sandals, purse, necklace, "here's the guy I was telling you about—Pete, Pete Minelli the brain. Remember I told you about Pete. So—didja become a college professor or what?"

"High school teacher," Daddy answers without apology or pride. He's retired now. Sometimes when I come home from the city to visit him, people still stop me on the street to tell me he was their teacher. He taught for forty-three years. His final yearly paycheck was sixty-two thousand dollars. Two thousand dollars more than my first royalty advance.

"This is my daughter," Daddy says to Bob, and then to several others who gather around. Suddenly he's the center of attention. I haven't see Daddy draw a crowd like this in a couple of years, not since the Christmas he tried on all his presents at once, then did a comic striptease right down to his boxer shorts. The rare strain of exhibitionism has always been a surprising element of Daddy's quiet makeup. The sort of thing I wonder whether he showed more of when he was young—before I was born.

"My daughter," he says again and again. His hand on my elbow is hot and dry.

"You a brain, too?" someone asks jovially. "Must be if you're a writer. Ever been on TV?"

Yes. I tell them about a talk show I taped this very morning in New York.

"Don't get that show in Denver," one of the women says. I've forgotten that, unlike Daddy, most of these people have long ago moved away from their hometown, this pretty, sleepy little city nestled in the hills of south-central New York State. Mark Twain country, they call it now that Madison Avenue has had a go at southern New York tourism.

"Nope, never heard of that show," someone else remarks. "Can you use another beer, Pete?"

An hour later, Daddy's still surrounded, but I've snuck away toward the table in the corner for a rest from the smiling. I'm trying to be inconspicuous and nearly succeeding when a lone man, playing a loud, strange song on a harmonica suddenly stands beside me. His clothes are impeccable and his hair is thick and black, but his whole body seems wrinkled—scuffed. "Who are you?" he asks, his lips leaving the harmonica for the briefest of moments.

"Pete Minelli's daughter."

"You a brain, too?"

"I…"

"Listen—" he begins, "I've done a lot in these last fifty years, don't think I haven't. I've played this thing all over America. Been on talk shows in New York City…."

Before I can say a thing, I feel my father's hand at my elbow again. "Time to go, honey," he says, nodding to the harmonica-player. "Nice to see you again, Ben."

"More than one kind of brain in this world, Minelli," Ben cryptically remarks as Daddy leads me toward the door.

When we exit, the chairman, who's still standing guard, hands him a newspaper-wrapped package the size of a football.

"Mango," the chairman says. "Sam Matthews grows 'em down in Florida. Didn't want to leave them down there to rot, so he brought 'em along. Free of charge, Pete."

"Thanks," Daddy says, his smile a little tired. "Thanks a lot. See you tomorrow."

"You like mangoes, Dad?" I ask.

"Don't know," he says. "Never tasted one."

When we get back to the house, we share the mango. "Looks good," he says, carefully slicing the bright orange flesh of the fruit. I watch his hand. All his life Daddy has been a neat, precise man. I have to think hard to remember ever seeing him dirty. But when I do remember, the images come flooding back. Daddy paint-spattered every October, tackling some portion of the house. Daddy in greasy coveralls fixing his car. Daddy covered in sawdust, soil, snow…

When we finish, he rinses the knife, swipes the tabletop with a damp cloth. He disappears into the family room and comes out with his high-school yearbook.

"Here," he says softly, "is the real brain of the class—" His finger, slightly bent with arthritis, rests near a photo of a girl who was seventeen then, half a century ago. Out of her eyes shines unmistakable intelligence and an innocent beauty that takes my breath away. "Alice Tunbridge Smith," Daddy says with respect. "Her average was three-quarters of a point higher than mine."

"Show me you, Dad," I ask, and he flips the stiff pages, releasing the slight odor of mildew. Beneath his picture, one I've seen many times before, is a quote. "Born to excel."

"Everybody got a slogan," Daddy says. "Some people lived up to theirs; some didn't."

"Did you, Dad? Did you excel?"

"Sure," he says, smiling at me. "Sure I did."

Next day there's an autumnal haziness to the air, but the temperature is in the nineties. Daddy and I are standing on the steps of a small, enclosed wooden gazebo on the campus of Elmira College staring in the window. Inside are Mark Twain's typewriter, his chair, his cot, even a pile of notes for a book. A small sign reminds visitors that in this little octagonal building he wrote what lots of people still think is the best American novel ever published.

"Used to be right smack on top of a hill," Daddy tells me. "When he wrote Huck Finn, he could stare out for miles. But there was another building up there on his in-laws' land—a cabin for his kids and their cousins, I guess. Your grandfather told me that it was deserted when he was a boy but that you could go to the main house and they'd give you a key. It had a fireplace and my father said the boys used to cook potatoes up there." He smiled as if an old memory had just struck him. "Alice Smith wrote a paper about it once and got one hundred per cent."

We stroll the grounds. I must have visited this campus with Daddy a hundred times—it's one of his favorite places. He steers me toward an exhibit hall. The walls of the large room are lined with photos of Twain and of scenes from his colorful life. I'm studying a panel depicting life on the Mississippi river boats and reading how Twain chose his pen name, which, the caption tells me, means "safe water," when Daddy plucks at my sleeve. "Look at this, honey…this is probably one of the kids that cabin was built for."

The picture shows a tiny girl in a stiff, lacy pinafore. The caption beneath tells how once this same little girl went flying down a hill in her baby carriage because her father had let go of it to light his cigar….

"He was a bum. A regular bum. A lot of writers are, and Twain's no exception," Daddy comments later. It's afternoon and we're sitting on the patio of the Andersons. They went to school with Daddy, too. Mrs. Anderson has read every one of my books. She has me sign a pile, then brings out her scrapbook to show me her own brushes with fame. Her daughter dressed as a butterfly for a PTA performance, her son's piano recital, a photo of the day she won a horticultural prize at the state fair in Syracuse…and a picture of that strange man with his harmonica.

"Who's that?"

"Ben Long—the class clown. Moved to New York. Too bad about Ben. He was so clever," Mrs. Benson sighs. "But he never amounted to anything. He lives at the Y or something like that. If he ever had a wife, she's long gone now. No kids. Speaking of kids…" Now Mrs. Anderson is showing me a studio portrait of seven young people. Daddy smiles politely and has to tell her he has no grandchildren. She looks at me for an instant. Frowns.

The official reunion dinner that night is elegant. At first Daddy and I sit nervously alone at a table set for eight, but soon it begins to fill up. An exceptionally flirtatious retiree takes the place beside me. I stifle laughter at his slightly suggestive jokes, uncomfortable until his wife winks and says, "He's been like that for fifty years…." When I look up from this exchange, I see that a trim, lovely woman has taken the seat beside Daddy. With a soft warmth to his voice he introduces her.

"This is Dr. Alice Smith. She is a professor at Columbia."

Daddy's tone is wistful. Is he envious? Who wouldn't be? Does he still harbor guilt all these years later that his principal decided it would be better to have a male valedictorian than a female?

Suddenly I realize that perhaps it is I who is envious, but I have no time to explore the thought for my father is saying, "and this is my daughter, Teresa, a fine writer."

We chat. We eat. At the very next table sit six of Daddy's grade-school teachers. In their midst is Ben Long, regaling them with stories about his adventures as a harmonica player. The teachers smile and nod, their white heads still teacherly, their old fingers patiently lifting silverware that seems immensely large in their hands.

Soon it's time for the awards—small trophies with a golden wreathed number fifty atop a marble base. The oldest—one of the teachers, of course. The youngest—I know a moment's fear, but soon realize only people associated with the school are contenders. The most children. The one who's come the farthest—the mango man wins here. The most successful: Columbia Professor Alice Smith and musician Ben Long, who, the chairman announces, "has always done things his own way...."

Daddy sits quietly through all this, smiling, applauding, thinking his own thoughts.

At the end, we all stand, hold hands and sing the school song. Alice Smith has tears in her eyes. The man next to me is making a suggestive gesture against my palm. Daddy is squeezing my fingers too tightly. And I, of course, am faking the words.

The next morning, I have to leave early, but Daddy insists on taking me to breakfast at a restaurant atop one of the hills. Afterwards, we stare down at the hazy city nestled in its sleepy valley. "Daddy," I ask, "do you think Mark Twain really was a bum?"

He hesitates. He turns to me with a grin that's the closest to mischievous that Daddy can get. "Sure he was. He lived off his in-laws. He played pool all day. He sat up here in the hills all summer and daydreamed year after year…. But he brought a lot of pleasure to a lot of people—showed them things they'd have never seen otherwise."

In silence we stare out at the scene. After what seems a long time, Daddy says, "It made me proud to have you here, Teresa. Far as I'm concerned, Ben Long and Alice Smith got nothing on me."

He turns and I kiss him softly on the cheek. The moment is so poignant I'm almost afraid one or both of us is going to cry. But neither does. I smile. Daddy winks. "Born to excel," he declares, his words too close and low to echo from the hills. He glances out over them one more time. Then he takes my hand and together we head back to his car.

THE TOY

I am number 3214-19-4853972AF-61. I been that number since I got to be three years old and didn't have to work outside in the fields anymore and could come into the factory.

Now I been in the factory for four years and we make toys. There are trucks and games and guns and especially dolls. My job is to run the machine that puts the clothes on the dolls before another machine puts the dolls in boxes.

So I get to be the last one to work on the doll before it's done.

This isn't hard. The machine is very fast and does the job by itself. All I have to do is make sure the dress on the doll is folded tight so that it will go in the box without any trouble.

In the years I been working in the factory, I seen lots and lots of beautiful dolls.

For my own, I only have a doll made for me by my grandmother before she had to be taken to the old people place. It's from a spare towel we had once and my grandmother made arms and legs and a nice face and even hair.

I like to play with my doll, but I can't help it, I always think about the girls who get to play with the dolls we make in the factory. I heard that all these toys—and especially the dolls—go to another country where every girl has a whole lot of dolls and sometimes even throws them away when she doesn't feel like playing with them anymore.

Maybe I was thinking about that the day one of the dolls I was working on got caught in the machine and her yellow dress got ripped.

The big machine stopped. The mistake bell rang so loud I thought that the guards would come running.

But I thought I was lucky because only two came. One of them was a young man with a real mean face. When I saw him looking at me, I was sure I was going to be punished. Maybe even sent downstairs.

I never been downstairs. And I don't know what happens there because I heard of a lot of workers who were sent down but I don't know any who ever came back.

Anyway. He just looked at me, the mean one, and then he clicked some keys on his hand computer. I don't know what it said. Maybe my number or the number of the machine. Maybe he subtracted one from the number of dolls. I just don't know.

Then the other one came, with a smile on his face, but scary anyway. He picked up the doll with the ripped yellow dress. He pulled the dress up away from the doll's legs, and he put his hand computer near the back of the doll where the secret code was. Then he nodded his head to the other man and they both started to walk away.

I waited for a couple of minutes. Nothing happened. I just stood there. I was afraid the camera would pick me up and the supervisor would see that I wasn't moving. I looked behind me to see if she was coming.

And when I did, I saw that the mean-looking man had the doll in his hand. I was sure he was going to bring it to the office, sure I would be punished.

But he stopped at the discard barrel, passed his computer over the code on the doll's back one more time, then tossed it into the barrel. He had to press the lid hard because the barrel was so full. Then together with the other guard, he walked away.

I worked my whole shift. Nobody came near me. Nobody asked any questions. I thought I wasn't in any trouble. I was extra careful with everything and nothing else went wrong.

Except that when I left my station and turned around to head to the locker room, I saw that something was sticking out of the trash barrel and that the men hadn't come yet to empty it for the day.

I guessed that hard as they had pressed, the top hadn't been pushed down all the way after all.

I knew I shouldn't have touched it, but I also knew the "bad" doll was in there. I looked around. Everybody was lining up for the end of our shift, waiting to be clocked out. There were lots of girls near me, but they were pushing and shoving to be first in line and not have to wait for the whole crowd of us to be processed. Nobody was looking at me.

So I did it. I pushed the lid of the garbage barrel just a little bit aside. And I reached in and I grabbed the yellow cloth and I pulled the doll out of the barrel.

Of course I had to hide it and fast. If anybody saw me, I would be sent downstairs for sure. And I had to hide it not just from people who could see it, I also had to hide it from the checkers at the door.

I almost gave up. I almost threw the doll to the ground and pretended I didn't know anything about it.

But then I got an idea.

There was a big crowd waiting in line to get out, to get checked and then to leave and go to the dormitories. There was such a crowd that people were standing really close together. So close that if I was careful, I could wait until someone ahead of me was checked and allowed to go through and then I could put the doll somewhere on them, get checked myself, then take the doll back before anybody could figure out what I was doing.

I wanted to make sure that I could do this without getting anyone else on my team in trouble. Just to make sure, I wanted to be next to somebody that I didn't know. This wasn't as hard as it might seem. There were hundreds of girls working on a lot of teams and there were also three other factories whose shifts ran at the same time as ours every day—and night, too, though I wasn't yet old enough to do the night shift.

I pushed through the crowd, being very careful. If I made a mistake and either of us were caught with the doll, I couldn't say what would happen. We all knew stories about girls who had done something wrong, even some little thing like going to the wash station instead of coming straight back from our ten-minute daily break. Those girls were never seen again – or so people whispered.

Anyway, I did it. I watched. I lined up behind the girls who were passing through the least scary of the guards. Everybody knew that he smiled a lot of times and that he wasn't rough when he felt us all over to see if we were taking anything out of the factory.

At first I didn't think I could put the doll anywhere on the girl ahead of me without her feeling what I was doing. I decided just to drop the doll and to step on it so that it would get at least a little crushed and maybe not look like a doll any more. I had almost decided this when the line moved forward fast all of a sudden.

Before I even had a chance to move, I got pushed from behind and the doll fell out of my hand. I thought I was finished.

But then a miracle happened.

Instead of falling to the ground, the doll slipped away and got caught in the uniform apron of the girl in front of me. I held my breath. I figured the guard would see it and she would get in trouble. I felt bad about this. As I said, I never meant to get anybody else in trouble.

I drew in a big breath.

And the guard heard me. "Something wrong?"

I shook my head. I thought he would pat all my clothes, the way he always did. But instead, he shook his head and made a sign with his hand that it was okay for me to move on.

By the time I caught up with the girl that was in front of me, the doll was gone. I didn't know whether to be happy or sad.

We were almost back to the dormitory when the girl looked around to make sure nobody was watching, reached under her apron and pulled out the doll. She handed it to me without saying a word. Then she turned and walked away so fast that I couldn't say a word to her, either.

The doll's dress was torn more than it was before and there was dirt on the dress and on the face of the doll and the hair was pulled out of the ribbons that held it before.

But I didn't care. I put it under my own apron and when I got to my cot, I put it under the sheet.

I went to supper and to our exercises and our confessions and I went to bed. But I didn't go to sleep. Under the blanket on my cot, I played with my doll. I couldn't say anything in case somebody could hear me.

But I could pretend without saying anything. I pretended I lived in the place that the other girls lived—the place where they had all the dolls they wanted. The place where they could throw a doll away if they got tired of playing with it. The place where they had a whole lot of dolls and not just one and not one that was dirty and torn.

I pretended I had pretty clothes myself and that I didn't have to work in the factory and that I could live with my mother—or even just know who she was.

And I pretended that my doll was perfect. And that she could talk and tell me things about the place where she lived.

And I pretended that she could sing and dance and say my name.

And I pretended that I didn't hear the boots on the stairs.

And I pretended that I didn't hear the loud knock on the door.

MERRY CHRISTMAS, DEAR ORPHANS

As I sit here wrapping a gift to donate to my church's collection of presents for children who can't afford books, I suddenly recall the Christmas, sixty years ago, when the girls from my grade four class visited the orphanage in Buffalo.

Now all during our childhood we had been warned that if we didn't behave we would end up at Father Baker's. I know now what I didn't know then. Far from being a tyrant who punished children relentlessly, who harbored delinquent fugitives, who was a figure whose abode was to be avoided at all cost, Father Baker was a saintly man who had died long before. His work rescuing abandoned children, at a time when thousands of infant bones from babies cast away by unwed mothers, were found in the waters off Buffalo, eventually led to the founding of institutions for the homeless and destitute that still serve Buffalo today.

So we had to be reassured that we were not going to *that* orphanage but to another where innocent little girls who had lost their parents—we assumed though death—were living peacefully under the watchful guidance of faithful and gentle nuns like our own teachers.

We started to get ready before Thanksgiving. We had lots of meetings. Being only nine years old or so, we had never been to a meeting except for Girl Scouts. Our trip to Buffalo, our helping those whom we came to consider "the poor" seemed far more important than learning how to tie knots or bake pies, which we did at Scouts.

Now I had never seen a poor person, let alone an orphan. I knew that in different parts of Niagara Falls where we lived there were "bad" neighborhoods. And some of the girls at school wore the same dress every time we were allowed to be out of our uniform. But that was about the extent of my experience of people whose means were far less than my own.

I have to admit, I didn't know any rich people, either. Sometimes on Sunday after church, my father would take us for a drive. We passed big, fancy houses in Lewiston or on Grand Island, but the only one we ever went into belonged to my Uncle Sammy, whose real name was Salvatore and who looked like a genuine Italian with a little mustache and of whom I was completely afraid. I don't remember why.

Anyway, at our meetings we discussed people who had less than us and what they might like that we could give them. We talked about clothes, but how could we know the sizes? We talked about candy and other things to eat, but how would we find out what was allowed in the institution? And we talked about books. To me, that seemed a very exciting gift, but a lot of the others thought that would be boring and that giving books would be like suggesting that the orphans should be working harder in school.

In the end, we settled on dolls. My mother made a beautiful outfit for the doll I was to bring. It was red velvet, a gown with a cape that had a hood made of fake white fur. It had a matching purse and little red shoes that she made by covering the doll's feet with fabric. I was almost sad to wrap this doll because I was so proud of the beautiful job my mother had done that I didn't want to hide it with tissue paper. All the way to Buffalo, I held it in my lap and when we got to the orphanage, I was still holding it.

The orphanage must have been the biggest building I had ever seen. I thought it looked like a castle. It was red stone with towers and balconies and a driveway that curved up from the street under a wide canopy of what looked like carved stone.

The noisy chatter that had accompanied us all the way from Niagara Falls fell into a hush as we pulled up to huge wooden doors like the ones we'd seen in storybooks about Cinderella the night she met the prince. These doors were carved like the canopy was with clouds from which angels peeked at all who entered.

As we stood in awe, Sister Mary Martha, the day's leader of our journey, reached as high as she could, took in her small hand a huge brass circle from its resting place on the door, then let it down with a resounding smack.

Now of course we had been prepared in what we thought was every way for this mission of mercy. We stood in two straight and silent lines while we waited for what seemed like eternity before the door creaked open and Sister Mary Martha's Buffalo twin nun stood there, smiling and beckoning us in.

We expected to be impressed by the size and ornate decoration of the huge wood-clad hall. We were. We expected to be charmed by a giant Christmas tree covered with lights and ornaments. We were. We expected to be welcomed by five or six friendly nuns. We were. We expected to see lines of uniformed girls standing in an orderly display of welcome and—of course—gratitude. We didn't.

Instead, before we could even get our bearings in the large and forbidding hall, we heard the racket of yelling voices, the pounding of eager feet down some long hallway. And then we felt it. Countless hands pulling each of us from different directions, girls screaming as they grabbed at our clothes, knocked us off balance and—above all—scrambled to get hold of the packages we carried.

Shocked, we stood still, though our hostesses, twenty little girls with the power of a multitude, swarmed around us, taking everything we had: the gifts we had so carefully wrapped, the "refreshments" we had discussed for so many weeks.

Our daintily frosted cookies were jammed into mouths when they weren't being fought over and landing on the floor that, absurdly, I noticed was made of beautiful marble stars and crosses in all sorts of shades of pale red, gold and gray.

Sister Mary Martha clapped her hands. It took us a minute to recognize the sound but when we did, we lined up as we had rehearsed, getting out of the way of flying cookies, discarded wrapping paper, already broken dolls, ripped books, a couple with their covers torn off.

I had only a second to look down before I had to pay attention to Sister Martha's conducting of our tiny choir. Before I did, I saw two orphans struggling between them for the doll that I had brought. Without thinking that I would get into trouble, I reached for my mother's creation and yanked it from their hands.

It was too late. Already the red velvet dress was ripped; one of the little red shoes my mother had so carefully sewn was gone.

I felt like crying.

This was so different from what I had expected. Where were the angelic orphan faces? Where was the gratitude? Where was the honor we should have had because we had thought about somebody else's needs instead of our own?

I tried hard to sing the Christmas carols, but all I could think about was how awful the orphans were. Even now, instead of singing with us, they were gobbling sweets and arguing over who had seen what first.

Each of them seemed to have an armful of items.

It wasn't until we finished singing—and also praying—and were zipping up our coats that I saw a tiny girl sitting on the floor by the door. This orphan had empty arms. All the stronger, braver girls would have taken away anything she might have gotten her hands on.

As I passed the little girl--our neat line now headed for our bus-- I leaned down and handed her the doll with the ripped red dress and the single shoe.

She stopped crying. She stared at this gift. A look I couldn't read passed her young face.

She looked up at me. I couldn't read her expression. But whatever it had been, it suddenly changed to a look of fury. She grabbed the doll and she threw it at me as hard as she could.

All the way back, I tried to hide the fact that I was crying. And when I got home, I had to hide the fact that the beautiful doll my mother had dressed was now hidden in my coat.

It stayed there for a very long time, until it, and the true story of the trip to the orphanage were forgotten.

Until today.

I thought those awful little girls who grabbed our gifts with such abandon were greedy. I thought they lay in wait for us, like an ambush. I thought they didn't appreciate all we had done for them.

But when I look back now, I wonder. Was their explosive response to our well-meant kindness greed?

Or was it a kind of joy?

ROSEMARY AUBERT

TAKING OFF

I only signed up because my husband was constantly on my back to do something "meaningful" with my retirement.

It had been a couple of months since I'd left the library. As much as I had enjoyed most of my career, which had been spent with the silent companionship of thousands of perfectly arranged books, I was getting fed up by the end.

Quiet had become a thing of the past with noisy school groups and old people's book clubs and so-called "clients" (which used to be "readers") talking to each other or listening to music through ear-phones that never quite cut out the sound that was supposed to be private.

Not to mention the fact that books were constantly "disappearing", were being dumped wherever the reader happened to be when he or she lost interest. In fact, it was pretty clear to me that books were just about to go the way of the dodo bird—not that anybody remembered what that meant.

So the minute I could get my full pension, I fled.

The two or three months I'd spent at home had been wonderful. Gardening, cooking. No pressure. No expectations.

"Look," my husband said, "these sound interesting." He attempted to hand me a fistful of brochures that I was sure featured all kinds of "activities". I didn't want an activity. I wanted peace and quiet in my own home.

"I'm beating eggs for meringue for the lemon pie," I said. "I'll look at them later."

He nodded and put them down on the coffee table in the living room where I would see them when I passed by—

spread out in a nice fan-shape on the table top. One thing I found I could finally do now that I didn't have a job was to dust the furniture on a regular basis. The first couple of times had been challenging. It's amazing how dust piles up after a month or so.

The pie was delicious. One good thing about being an inveterate reader is that you can follow instructions with no trouble. My husband loved the pie. He loved it enough to have a couple of pieces with a nice cup of tea, a snack that made him sleepy. When he woke up from his nap, he'd forgotten all about the brochures.

After I'd done the dishes, scoured the stove and sponged out the microwave, I sat down for a brief rest in the living room. My eye fell on the fan of brochures.

There was one from the university. The continuing education courses offered there sounded intimidating, even guilt-instilling. "How will we save the earth from the damage of carbon? Join this discussion on a weekly basis to learn our fate and our responsibility."

No thanks. I didn't want to learn how to save the earth or write a novel or do beginning calculus or study the historical implications of immigration.

I took a look at pamphlets from the so-called "community colleges". These courses were sure not to have any papers or exams or deep "discussions" about the fate of the world. Or so I thought.

"Multicultural quilting. Learn to sew the new history of Canada." No. "Writing your life. See how journaling can help you live more fully." No. "Recycling. Saving our children's future." No. No children.

I was about to throw the whole lot into, yes, the recycling bin, when my eye fell on one that I had missed. It wasn't slick like the brochures from the university and the colleges with their colorful photos of happy, fulfilled students. In fact, it looked like somebody had produced it on their own computer.

This school seemed without a name, but it did have an encouraging slogan, "Learn from the experts." It featured only four courses. One was about how to get a job at the doughnut shop of your choice. Two others were about wise grocery shopping and getting the best value at the pharmacy.

I almost tossed this pamphlet too.

Then my eye caught the title of the fourth course: "Taking off: Learn to love your body with tips from a professional."

Now, a woman my age—that is to say on the wrong side of sixty—has pretty much come to terms with her shape. It had been a long time since I'd believed that I could do anything—beyond modest exercise and a "responsible" diet to become, as the course outline promised, "more positive and accepting about the way you look."

The course was only four weeks long, four Tuesday mornings, and it wasn't on any university or college campus. It was down the street at the community centre.

I decided to go for it, just in case my husband asked.

As it turned out, he saw me writing the cheque. He peeked over my shoulder to see to whom it was made out. "Wonderful," he said. "Not that there's anything wrong with your body."

I smiled. I didn't say what I was thinking, which was *I guess we're going to see about that.*

The first few minutes of the first class were spent on the ten participants introducing themselves to each other. They were, for the most part, oldish women. A couple of them looked like they'd signed a life contract with the purveyor of white-haired puffed up hairdos that could last a week without shampooing. And a couple others looked like old hippies who'd never quite made the leap into the present. And the rest looked like me. Nondescript. Decent but nothing to write home about as they had all been used to saying in their youth.

And then there was the "professional".

Now of course I had checked the brochure to see what kind of professional this woman was supposed to be. It said that she had been in the entertainment field for a number of years and that she was now devoting her time to helping the "mature" woman come to a happy "partnership" with her "changing" body.

Sounded okay to me. And she looked okay. At first. Her hair was a little brassy and a whole lot more abundant than that of her students, rising, then falling in a cascade of wild auburn curls. And she was clearly a fan of Avon and its competitors—lots of eye makeup and those red lips that looked like they'd been painted on by one of the students in the "Capturing the human face in art" classes.

She was wearing a sort of trench coat. Nothing odd about that. It was, after all, the spring semester, which put us at the top end of the new season.

But when she took the coat off, I realized that there are a lot of branches of the entertainment industry and that I was about to become familiar with one that I had never fully—or even sketchily—investigated before.

She was wearing shorts. I mean really short shorts. I would put her at around forty, but judging from everything that was visible below her waist, her changing body didn't need much in the way of partnership. She looked terrific with long, strong legs and, sorry to have to say it, a butt that you could bounce a coin off of.

And that was only half of it. The upper half was also available for view. She wore a tight black top that matched the shorts in more ways than one. For example, you could see as much of her top as you could see of her bottom.

As I was getting used to this outfit and wondering what it had to do with coming to grips with my own body, she took a laptop computer out of big leather bag she was carrying, set it on the desk and pressed a few keys.

I wasn't expecting the Toronto Symphony Orchestra. After all, this wasn't "Music for mental growth," this was "Taking off…" The music was a pounding relentless beat that instantly called to mind a whole slew of clichés, none of them reminiscent of hymns.

I realized at once the stupid mistake I'd made. My husband was a retired insurance salesman. He was always telling me how much trouble people could get into by not making sure of the exact meaning of a word or a phrase.

There was only one thing to do. I stood up, retrieved my jacket from the back of my chair, picked up the notebook I was now embarrassed to have opened with naïve eagerness and headed for the door.

"What's the matter, honey?" the teacher said.

I froze in my tracks. What was I supposed to say? That I'd never seen a stripper in person before? That I'd been so eager to do what my husband wanted me to do that I'd made a fool of myself? How about that I was such a prude that the idea of learning anything from an "exotic dancer" wasn't something I'd ever sully myself by doing?

I glanced at the other students. They were all staring at me as though I were deserting a sinking ship and leaving all of them to fend for themselves.

"I—I… I have to put money in the parking meter."

Great. Now I was not only a student of strip tease, I was also becoming a liar.

"Hurry back, honey," the teacher said sweetly. "You don't want to miss anything. We're going to get going on the moves in a few minutes."

One of the other students winked at me. I thought she had a hell of a nerve. The gesture, tiny as it was, changed my mind about the rest of the day's lesson. I wasn't a wimp. I wasn't a chicken. If all these other old ladies could do the moves, why couldn't I?

"I'll be right back," I said.

I had to hide in the washroom on another floor until enough time had passed to make it look like I'd actually gone down to the street. Then I summoned my courage and went back to class.

Well, the moves were pretty entertaining. Imagine fifteen sixty-five-year olds gyrating. I had no choice but to gyrate, too.

I guess we kept it up for forty-five minutes or so, before the teacher, who told us her name was Fancy, called a break, followed by a power point presentation on the history of exotic dancing. I was ready to sit down. I fell asleep for a few seconds, but on the whole, I learned more than I ever imagined there was to learn about what Fancy called, "a real art".

"That's it for today, ladies," she said. Did I mention that it was only women attending the class? In this day and age, it was considered completely incorrect to make any assumptions about gender. So had I known what I was in for, I wouldn't have assumed that there would be no men present. Nonetheless, I was saved at least that little embarrassment.

"Good work, girls," Fancy said. "I'll see you next week. Oh, and be sure to wear a top that buttons down the front."

When I got home, my husband was sitting in the living room reading, deeply absorbed in whatever was on the screen of his tablet. It took him a couple of minutes to finish, to look up and ask me, "Well, how did it go? Did you discover any secrets about yourself today?"

He smiled sweetly, stood, gave me a kiss on the cheek. "Whatever you discovered," he said, "I'm sure it'll be something nice."

"Yes," I said. "Want some supper?"

The next week, we practiced taking off our tops. We were all pretty pathetic at first, but between the helpful music and the enthusiastic coaching of Fancy, we were what she called amateur professionals after about an hour or so. I learned how to tease a button. I learned how to slither a sleeve. I learned how to move back to front, front to back, each time lowering my blouse a tiny bit until, by the end of the recording, it fell smoothly to the floor, leaving me in my fortified bra and my polyester slacks.

"Be sure to wear slacks that zip up the front—or jeans, or you can change into shorts," were Fancy's parting words for the week.

Which is where my nun-school underpants came into play.

To make a long story short, I got through the whole course—all four classes—without missing a beat—so to speak. In fact, by the end of the third class, I was actually having fun. The only thing missing was a male audience. The other old ladies in the class joked a lot and we had a good time, but underlying everything was the fact that our only audience was Fancy and ourselves.

"What you have to do soon as you can," Fancy advised, "is practice at home right away. If you don't dance for somebody soon, you're going to forget and you're going to lose all the work we did."

I thought about that. My husband wasn't home when I got there, which gave me time to get ready. I couldn't do anything about the fashionless underwear I'd worn all my life, but I could and did put the disc I'd bought from Fancy in the last moments of our time together on the stereo, ready to play the minute he came in the door.

Fortunately, I didn't have to wait long. Within minutes, I was sliding and gesturing and slithering and piling my clothes in a sweet little heap on the floor until there was nothing left to take off.

With what I thought was a flirtatious look, I glanced up at my husband.

He was standing stock still, a look of complete shock on his face. He wasn't smiling. He wasn't frowning. In fact, he wasn't breathing.

Neither was I.

Finally, he drew in a shaky gasp.

"What time," he asked "is supper?"

That night we made love as we always did on Tuesday. It wasn't any different than any other time. I soon began to think that I was supposed to forget the whole night school thing and go back to my usual pre-adult education hobbies. I was about equally relieved and disappointed.

I guess it was three days later that my husband came home with a present for me. It was a box wrapped in flowered paper and when I opened it, I found a nice new pair of gardening gloves and then a gluten-free recipe cookbook. I thought that was all, but then I noticed a slim little package at the bottom of the box, wrapped in pink tissue paper.

As I opened it, my fingers shook a little. I pulled aside the tissue and I found a black lace bra. I smiled with delight. Never in all our years together had my husband given me any such thing.

But that wasn't all.

There was one more item.

Underpants.

Bikini underpants.

THE CANADIAN CAPER

At it again!

Mrs. DiRosa manoeuvred her walker so that it was flush against the sill of the hallway window on the sixth floor of The Towers—called Wobble Towers by her smarty-pants grandchildren. It was the only way she could free both hands in order to adjust her binoculars. *Damn cheap things. If they made them here, instead of some foreign country, they'd work better.*

She fiddled with them until she could see the Canadian flag clear as a bell on the other side of the river. That was one of the things her daughter said was so great about The Towers. That you could get such a good view of the bridge from Niagara Falls, New York to Niagara Falls, Canada.

"Could be the only place in the world where you can look out a window and see another country," her helpful son-in-law had suggested when they'd signed her in.

Big deal!

She trained the binoculars on a vehicle stopped at the Canadian toll booth and gave the focus knob one more little shove. *Good thing I don't have arthritis!* She tracked the long truck full of logs as it slowly made its way through the narrow entrance and onto the bridge.

"You still looking at them trucks?"

At the squeaky-voiced question coming from behind, Mrs. DiRosa jumped a mile. She let the binoculars fall back around her neck by their cord and grabbed her walker, turning to face the only person she could stand in The Towers, her friend Meenie—or Teenie Meenie as Mrs. DiRosa's grandchildren called their grandmother's seventy-five-pound friend. Her real name was Minette, and a long time ago she'd left her home in Canada to live with her children before she, too, had been sent to The Towers. She still spoke with a French Canadian accent.

"What do you have to sneak up on me like that for?" Mrs. DiRosa said irritably. "Scared the dickens out of me and messed up my focus, too."

"You still watchin' them truckloads of frogs?"

"Logs, you silly old thing. Not frogs, logs."

"So why you watchin' them now?" Meenie asked.

"Look," Mrs. DiRosa said, forgetting her disgruntlement and eager to share her remarkable discovery. "See that truck coming through now?"

She handed the binoculars to Meenie who, being ten years younger, was more agile in every way and had no need of a walker to help her get close to the window. She held the binoculars to her eyes.

"Yeah, I see it," she said, "It just got to the American side. One of them nice-looking young men in the uniform is talking to the driver. So what?"

"Get a load of the very top log. See anything funny about it?"

Meenie was quiet for a few seconds. Studying. "I see a mark on the top log," she finally said. "A funny mark. Maybe like a hax hit it wrong."

"Axe," Mrs. DiRosa said. She had been correcting Meenie's English now for eighteen and a half years without any noticeable effect. "Yes, that's it."

"What's funny about a hax mark on a big log?"

"Nothing," Mrs. DiRosa said. "Except that I've seen that mark on that log six times since I started counting."

"What?"

"Meenie, that truck comes through here once every two weeks. And every single time, the same log is on top."

Meenie leaned closer to the window. "Comes down from Canada with the same log on top? I don't get it."

Mrs. DiRosa took the binoculars from her friend's hand. She trained them on the handsome young American customs official. She watched as he took a bunch of papers from the driver of the truck, glanced at them, nodded and waved the man on.

"They don't keep them long enough with nine-eleven and all," Mrs. DiRosa said. "No wonder there's so many smugglers."

Meenie laughed. "You read too many of them books. You got too much of imagination. There aren't smugglers now. That's stuff out of stories."

"No, it isn't," Mrs. DiRosa said, suddenly remembering bits and pieces of a conversation. "Somebody was talking about smuggling just last week."

Damn memory. Isn't worth a thing. Should have eaten more carrots or something.

Meenie thought about it for just a minute. "I know," she said. "It was at the Trans-border Social last Tuesday. You know, when those old ladies come over from Canada for lunch at The Towers."

"Yes, Meenie. You're right. That's it! They were talking about smuggling people out of foreign countries through Canada into the United States!"

"You don't think that truck of logs has people hid in it?"

Mrs. DiRosa took another look out the window. The log truck was just pulling onto the Parkway, headed for points south. "The logs could be hollow or something like that. I wouldn't be surprised. Foreigners are tricky. And getting into America is the thing they want most."

"But it's a big crime!" Meenie protested.

"Sure is," Mrs. DiRosa said. She caught one last glimpse of the truck as it disappeared down the highway. "A whole load of criminals headed right into the heart of America."

***

It wasn't until the next day that Mrs. DiRosa finally figured out what they had to do. "Meenie, you've got to talk to that nice young customs man."

Meenie laughed. "What I going to tell him—that my friend think people are coming in empty logs to America?"

"Don't be a smarty-pants. I'd do it myself only I can't walk. You can."

"But I can't talk that good. He won't listen. He'll just think I'm some old crazy person like Mr. Winters."

Mr. Winters no longer lived at The Towers because he'd wandered onto the bridge in his underwear on a February morning, swearing he was Canadian and wanted to die at home.

Meenie's got a point.

"OK," Mrs. DiRosa said, "I've got it. I'll write everything in a letter. How I've been watching the bridge for weeks now and have seen the same truck with the same logs go over time after time. I'll put in the letter about how I can see that top log from above, which is how I can tell it's the same log, when the customs men can't. Then they won't feel insulted or anything."

"Don't want to insult them, no," Meenie agreed.

"Then you'll do it?"

"To keep criminals out of America? OK."

It didn't take long to write the letter. Meenie was right about Mrs. DiRosa reading a lot of books. One thing it did for you was make it easy to write. She signed the letter, "An American Citizen." That sounded good.

Even though it would take Meenie a while to go all the way downstairs, then to the back door, then across the parking lot, then across the street, then onto the bridge and into the customs booth, Mrs. DiRosa got right up against the window the minute Meenie left her apartment.

It seemed to take forever before she finally caught sight of her. Luckily it wasn't a busy day on the bridge. Even without the binoculars, Mrs. DiRosa could see the customs man take the envelope from Meenie. She watched him tear it open and read the letter. Then she saw him step into the booth and pick up the telephone. She lifted the binoculars. Now she could see that the man was smiling and nodding. Was he talking to his boss? Were they going to check things out?

She waited for what seemed like a long time. Finally the man put down the phone. He stepped out of the booth. He had something in his hand, which he gave to Meenie. He was talking to her. Mrs. DiRosa couldn't see Meenie's face too clearly. But she did see that Meenie's shoulders were more slumped than usual. It didn't seem like a good sign. It wasn't a good sign either when the handsome young customs man patted Meenie on the head just like she was a dog.

***

"All he did was give me this," Meenie said, holding up a small, bright American flag.

"What did he *say*?" Mrs. DiRosa demanded. They'd already been through this several times, but she wanted to make sure.

"I *told* you," Meenie said, twirling the flag in her fingers until Mrs. DiRosa reached out and made her stop. "He say old ladies don't always see too good and not to worry because he's protecting America for us."

Mrs. DiRosa thought about it for one minute longer. Then she made up her mind. "That log truck has something wrong about it and I'm not going to give up until we find out what it is."

"How come you always say 'we'?" Meenie asked, beginning to twirl the flag again.

"There's only one thing *we* can do now," Mrs. DiRosa announced.

"Oh, no. What?"

"*We* have to go to Canada."

"But you can't even walk!"

"*We* will find a way."

"Stop saying we," Meenie said again, but of course, Mrs. DiRosa wasn't listening. She was thinking again.

***

The first thing they had to do was borrow a wheelchair from the office. It wasn't easy because for several years now, Mrs. DiRosa had told the The Towers' social worker that the only place she was going to be wheeled was to her grave.

"Where you be goin' then, sweetie?" the social worker asked. She was a nice young girl with a master's degree in social work from some university in Georgia.

Too bad they don't teach English in college any more. "To the library," Mrs. DiRosa lied, and Meenie, who was standing behind her, nodded.

"Well, you all be careful now, you hear?"

"Of course," both the old women said sweetly and simultaneously.

"Good, we fooled her," Mrs. DiRosa told Meenie as she got herself down into the chair and arranged a blanket around her legs. "Now we've got to get going. The plan's simple. We just wheel right on out the back door, over the parking lot, across the street—be sure to watch both ways—

and onto the bridge. On the American side we've just got to pay the toll—no questions asked. Once we get over to Canada, I'll tell them you don't speak any English. That way I can do all the talking."

"What if they find out we're missing from The Towers?" Meenie wasn't nearly as sure of the plan as Mrs. DiRosa.

"No problem. Today's Tuesday—Trans-border Social day. It's Canada's turn. I signed us both up. That bus driver's so lazy, he never checks how many there are. And if the Canadians have any questions, we just say we missed the Trans-border Social Club bus."

Meenie shook her head. "I don't think…"

"You don't have to think," Mrs. DiRosa said. "You just have to push."

***

It was cold going across the bridge even though it was the middle of June. The wind off the river smelled a certain way that Mrs. DiRosa remembered from long ago. It had been almost twenty years since she'd gone across the bridge in any way except by her daughter and son-in-law's car. She remembered Mr. DiRosa and all the times they went to Canada together in the old days, bringing back good Canadian tea, jam, cheese and toffee that killed your teeth and—for the Fourth of July—nice Canadian firecrackers that you had to hide under your blouse to get across. The memory of it made tears come to her eyes and the tears gave her a good idea.

"Don't say a thing, Meenie," Mrs. DiRosa reminded her friend as they came within a few yards of the Canadian customs booth. They could see the outline of a person behind the glass of the booth, but when the person stepped out with a little smile on her face, Mrs. DiRosa was surprised.

147

She'd expected the Canadian customs officer to be a handsome young man just like the American one. Only it was a young woman instead. A smart-looking young woman.

"Well now, ladies, what can I do for you?" the girl said. She looked friendly, but suspicious, too. Mrs. DiRosa was glad about the new angle to her plan.

She sniffled and squeezed her eyes shut, and made a few of the tears that were still in her eyes run down her cheeks. "I have come home to die," she said.

She could feel the back of the wheelchair wiggle a little bit, but Meenie kept her mouth shut.

The young woman looked shocked. "Come in here, ladies," she said, her voice a little shaky, "just wait for a moment, please."

She opened the door to the customs office. Meenie wheeled Mrs. DiRosa in. The customs officer disappeared down a narrow hall.

The minute she was out of sight, Meenie came around the front of the wheelchair. She was good and mad. "What's the matter with you?" she demanded of Mrs. DiRosa. "Why you tell them such a crazy thing? You want to be like Mr. Winters? How that fix the smugglers?"

"Calm down," Mrs. DiRosa said. "Remember how they got all those officials to come to the bridge when old Winters went crazy? They'll call the same ones now. The minute the bigwigs get here, we'll spill the beans."

They heard footsteps coming down the hall, the light steps of the female officer and then heavier steps.

"Here they come."

***

It was in all the papers: the *Niagara Gazette*, the *Buffalo Evening News*, even the papers up in Toronto and the *Pennysaver*. Mrs. DiRosa cut out the articles and taped them up on her wall. They showed her and Meenie talking to a reporter, and they said how they'd tipped off the bridge guards and broken up a ring of people smugglers.

Mrs. DiRosa's daughter was hopping mad at first. "I signed you up at The Towers so you would be safe, and look what you do—running off after smugglers."

"I didn't run after them, I just turned them in," Mrs. DiRosa said.

"Well, I'm taking those binoculars away right now. I don't want you to put yourself at risk like this ever again."

Mrs. DiRosa thought fast. "I'll give them in to the penny sale," she said. "Then somebody else can benefit by them."

Her daughter was about to answer that when the phone rang. It was a TV reporter from New York. She forgot about the binoculars when she found out Mrs. DiRosa was going to be on the news right across the country.

"You're hot now, Grandma," her grandchildren said when they heard that.

Smarty-pants.

Mrs. DiRosa manoeuvred her walker so that it was flush against the windowsill. She lifted the binoculars to her eyes.

"What you lookin' at now? More trucks?"

"'Course not," she said to Meenie. "I'm just checking to make sure these are all right before I give them in for the penny sale. You know how mad that social worker gets when people donate things that don't work."

Mrs. DiRosa leaned against the walker and freed her other hand to fiddle with the focus. She could see the Canadian flag clear as a bell across the river.

Good thing they teach people to respect their elders in Canada.

That's what she was thinking when she saw it again. Just as she had seen it twice before: a van driven by a man pulled into one of the parking lots a little ways down the river from the entrance to the bridge. The man seemed to disappear into the back of the van. Then after a little while, the front door of the van opened and a woman walked out. No sign of the man anymore. Like he had up and disappeared altogether. The woman walked toward the bridge, paid the toll and began to walk over the bridge right toward America.

"Lots of crooks in this world, Meenie," Mrs. DiRosa said.

"We gonna need that wheelchair again?" Meenie asked.
Could be, Meenie, could be....

THE PRIME SUSPECT

This story is dedicated to Professor Eric Mendelsohn of Ryerson University to whom I owe the premise.

A woman attempts to escape a plague and believes she has succeeded until she encounters the work of a trickster, showing, as in Day Eight of the Decameron, one of "those tricks which all people, men and women are playing upon each other all day long."

It spread like a plague. How else explain why it was everywhere?

She'd worked in a library all the years before her retirement, before she'd had time to take the math courses that were now her single pleasure. But even the library had been infected in the final years of her working there. That had been only five years before. Things had gotten a lot worse since then.

As she walked up St. George Street at the heart of the university, she felt the deadly enemy invade the very pores of her skin. Same as every day. Noise. The unavoidable, intrusive foe, like a virus or a bacteria. Like a cancer cell that multiplied with exponential efficiency. Cancer was considered an epidemic now, wasn't it?

Noise. She had no husband to wake up to anymore. Which was a tragedy. Because her Sam had been such a quiet man. She knew some women were cursed with husbands who snored. Thank heaven she had been spared that misery! When they had lived together in their beautiful house, she had awakened each day to the sound of exactly nothing. Not even the ticking of an annoying clock. Well, that was all changed now. That morning, like every morning, she had had to get up to the racket of the old-people's residence where she was trapped. Everybody who lived there but her was half deaf, and everything had to be turned up to top volume in order for her fellow residents to be able to hear what she could hear through the walls. Alarm clocks. The rush of water and the squeal of pressure in the pipes. The clink and clank of the heating system. The woman in the next room skyping to her sister in Bangladesh.

As she neared the Science Building, she gave wide berth to the vendors with their long lines of students waiting to buy the sort of things the kids liked to eat: French fries, shrimp rolls, hot dogs. She didn't mind the smell of these things, even at nine in the morning. What she hated was the sound of it all.

Their chatter seemed to comprise half the languages of the world, a sound like the buzz of a cloud of malaria-carrying mosquitoes. And the vendors themselves, calling out the orders for their foul-sounding wares: poutine, bratwurst, pho…

Worst of all was the music, if you could call it that. She had heard that a couple of math students had, as a semester project, figured out a trick to assign a musical tone to each numeral from. zero to nine. This meant that on their computers, their equations sounded like songs. Thankfully, not everyone in the math department had figured out how to do this, or the racket would have been even more unbearable than it was. Now: rap music; twanging squeaky female voices; young men engaging in an activity that they called singing, but which, to her, was nothing more than arrhythmic yelling. And then there was that Bieber kid and the guy from Korea that hopped around with his wrists crossed. And all of this leaking out of the little plastic gadgets called ear bugs—or something like that.

Shaking her head in annoyance—not that anybody was paying any attention to her—she climbed the steps of the Science Building. The wide glass door groaned as she pulled it open. Didn't anybody lubricate anything anymore? She made her way quickly through the groups of students gathered around the entrances to the classrooms and clustering on the stairs. Of course they couldn't hear her when she asked them to respect the safety regulations of the university by leaving stairwells clear of obstruction. The human voice, especially the voice of a small woman past the age of sixty, was as useless as the flu vaccine in July.

When she got to the fourth floor, she was relieved to realize that no one had got there before her, no one was going to give her a hard time about using the "Little Room".

Theoretically, continuing-ed students such as herself were not supposed to use the room, but she had gotten a special dispensation from her con-ed math professor, an intense, handsome, silver-haired man with dark eyes that sparkled whenever anybody asked him a question. Probably because it was rumoured that no one had ever asked him a math question that he couldn't answer. Anyway, the reason she was allowed to use the room was that after taking a decryption course from him, she had—all on her own—figured out how to decrypt the security device that kept the room locked. She did that now, her fingers on the keys fast so that any unauthorized person seeing her, either in person or by means of the video camera mounted in the hall, wouldn't have a chance of copying what she was doing.

She had to be careful. Because she needed the computer in that room. Her own little laptop just wasn't powerful enough for the equations she liked to play with.

And more importantly—most importantly, she needed the quiet so that she could concentrate.

Competition for the "Little Room" was so stiff that the story had gone around that a few years previously—before she'd entered the evening math program—a math student had been found murdered there, lying bloody on the floor between the computer and the door.

Of course, that had probably been an urban myth, though it was true that a student had died of some sort of heart failure somewhere in the Science Building. Well, that wasn't her problem. She set out her papers, signed in and got down to work.

It was fine. In fact, it was great. It was like going to the country when the racket in the city was starting to make you sick. There was simply nobody else around. For almost an hour, she worked away. It was a good day. The numbers she was playing with were co-operating beautifully. If she could keep on like this, she had a good chance of solving the set of linked equations that formed this year's math contest. The winner would receive a magnificent prize: A full year's expenses, including tuition, room and board—that is, the opportunity to become a matriculated mathematics student.

Fine at first. But after about an hour and a half, she thought she heard something. True, there was now the muffled buzz of students beginning to arrive for class, but that was one of the few sounds that didn't bother her, because everybody respected the "no-talking in the corridor" rule. Nobody wanted to be responsible for saying something or making a noise that might distract a fellow mathematician at the critical instant of insight that might enable that student to solve a problem he or she had been working on during their entire time at the university.

No. This was some other sound. Vaguely rhythmical. Not as insistent as rap or rock. Not as entwined and intriguing as classical. Musical, yes. But not any music she thought she'd ever heard before.

She was annoyed. Of course she was. But she would have been less the mathematician than she was if she had not been curious. Curious enough to leave her papers, the computer station, eventually the room itself in order to investigate.

When she opened the door, she could hear the sound much more clearly and now it had a dimensionality—that is, a direction.

She glanced down the hall. To the right was a single door that she knew led to a class always in session at this time of day. Basic Considerations of the Calculus. She didn't waste time going in that direction. There was no music there. At least not to her, though the professor of the course might disagree.

No. This was a real sound. This was noise and she set off in search of the source with the determination of an epidemiologist searching for the source of a virus.

Of course the more she moved in the direction of the strange tuneless, irregularly beating soundtrack, the louder it became.

Until she found herself in front of the door to the Number Theory Lab. She seldom bothered coming down here. She wasn't interested in number theory. In fact, it bored her, always looking at problems that she found too basic for consideration.

The sound was throbbing now. It seemed to increase in intensity moment by moment. There was no window in the door, so she had no idea which of her fellow math students was responsible for this disgusting intrusion into the silence of the building.

She knocked, but knew it could do no good. The sound coming from the room drowned out any other.

She tried the door knob, but of course the room was locked and coded, just as the little room had been.

It didn't take her long to decrypt the lock, but the sound, the wavering, sometimes repetitive, sometimes wildly divergent tones kept growing in intensity. Somebody had to be in there and somebody had to be told to stop that deadly, sickening noise.

After what seemed an eternity of seconds, the knob released and the door swung open.

Nobody. That's who she found in the room. Nobody.

And it was dark. The only light came from the screen of one of the computers ranged in a bank against the back wall, only about eight feet away. A dazzling, dizzying light that seemed to change color and intensity with every note that came out of the computer's speakers.

She wasn't entirely ignorant of number theory. She knew, for example, that there were classical searches. Infinite attempts to pin down some number that could never be found. The square root of two. The exact value of pi. And what this computer was looking for. The next prime number. The primes, the numbers divisible only by one and themselves. The numbers that stretched to infinity.

Someone had set this computer to that search and someone, some clever trickster, had set the search to music.

At first, she figured she could just turn it off. But the closer she got to the machine, the harder it became to move. Even a single step became too hard to manage. It was the number itself, as if it were some sort of animal that was defending itself against her. And its weapon was those dreadful sounds, those ringing notes that rang in a deafening cascade. There were thousands of primes, but so many had already been discovered that any new one might have thousands, even millions of digits. A million notes from a single numeral.

It was so loud that she couldn't think. Couldn't hear anything but the sound of the number. She raised her hands to shield her ears. And she felt a liquid flowing out of them. When she looked at her hands, she saw blood.

It was the last thing she ever saw.

THE MIDNIGHT BOAT TO PALERMO

What I loved most about meeting the midnight boat was not the motion of the waves, though I often thought the movement of the sea made it easier to sleep than the stillness of my bed. Nor was it the moonlight that I loved, for I was afraid of moonlight and am to this day. Many of the women in our self-help group speak of their fear of moonlight. Sometimes they connect it to abusive fathers or to their general terror of night. I loved my father and he never abused me in the way some of these women have been abused. But like them, talking now about my youth, I have stirred up a memory that I had buried long ago—forty years, in fact. I have suddenly understood that my father was murdered. I have suddenly remembered that I was there when he was killed. I have suddenly realized the name of his killer.

What I loved most about the midnight boat to Palermo was the silence. For my world, both then and now, has been a very noisy one. When I first came to this country, though I could not speak the language, I knew already that I spoke too loudly. How else could it be? There were, after all, seven of us, and we lived in a tiny hut on the shore of the inlet. We didn't call it an inlet, of course. That's a word I learned much later—in a writing class sponsored by the government. But an inlet it was, a little indentation in the rocks of the shore of Sicily. And when you spoke, if you were to be heard at all, you had to shout not only above the sound of all the brothers and sisters, not only above the arguing of my parents, but above the sound of the sea. That's what we called it. Not an inlet, the sea.

Like most of the people of our village, we were not rich. But we had plenty to eat and good clothes to wear, even though the Second World War had been over for only a few years. Twice a year, my mother would go to Rome and buy me and my sisters dresses, blouses with lace, shoes to wear to church on Sunday. Looking back on it now, it amazes me that we never questioned such extravagance. Nor did I question my mother's attitude about these trips. For weeks before, she'd be so sweet to us, so kind. Instead of her usual severity, she'd be almost gay. Though she said she hated to leave us, it was hard to ignore her happiness, just as when she returned, it was hard to ignore how angry she seemed to be for weeks. My mother, I thought then, was an unpredictable woman. But now I see, after all these years, she was far more predictable than I could have imagined.

When my mother was home, which was most of the time, she was a good mother. She sewed, she cleaned, and she made a tomato sauce that was famous in our little village. To this day, I can see her standing at the stove preparing it. She would start by heating a huge black iron pan and carefully dripping onto its hot surface a thin dribble of the purest olive oil. Then she would take a bud of garlic and carefully separating out each clove, would peel it with her slow, strong hands. When the heated oil had turned the garlic as golden as itself, she would add pieces of beef. This meat, too, would soon turn a golden color, filling our little house with its aroma. When the meat was done, she would add the tomato paste. It has been more than forty years since I have seen these things, but I remember as if I were standing there now how she would go to a little pantry off our kitchen, a place that was always cold, no matter the time of year, and from one of its shelves, would take an earthenware crock of tomato paste. This paste had been dried in the sun by her own grandmother, and it was almost black. Of course, I used to think it looked like poison. Yet even then I understood that the tomato paste made the sauce rich and thick and gave it such a deep flavor that it seemed to have been cooked forever. However, when she added this ingredient, my mother had to be very careful. If she added too much, or if she didn't cook it until it, too, was almost golden, the sauce would be bitter—a failure. After the tomato paste, the only other ingredient she added was fresh tomatoes. And one other thing—the secret. When the sauce had cooked for two hours, my mother would add a little cupful of sugar. It was my job to bring her the sugar from a cupboard across the kitchen, and I would sneak a taste for myself before I got to her side. When she caught me doing this, she would laugh.

Thursday was the day she made sauce. And Thursday was the night that it was my father's turn to meet the midnight boat to Palermo. I always thought that my father died on a Friday, but now I understand that was too simple a way to look at things. He was found dead on a Friday. He was killed on Thursday—the Thursday we, he and I, like always, were supposed to meet the Palermo boat but didn't.

My father, and all the other men in the village, worked in the sugar factory. Being only eight years old, I thought the factory had been there forever. Now I see that was wrong. It could only have been set up after the war, when I was two or three. When I was little, though, the sugar factory was one of the centers of my life. Though my own children seemed to spend all their time in school when they were eight years old, I certainly did not. There was only one teacher, an old woman whose son had gone away and never come back and who could speak of little else, even when she was supposed to be teaching us math or the history of the rulers of Sicily. It was easy to slip out of school—or not to go at all, which was what I often did. The minute I was free, I headed for the factory.

Now it is very important for me to explain that I did not go to the factory to eat the sugar. The mysterious thing about the factory was that nobody was ever allowed to eat the sugar there. Zi Antonio had forbidden it. Anyone who so much as tasted the tiniest bit would have to leave their work—forever. Zi Antonio was the mayor of our little village, though that word—mayor—is another that we never used, that I never even learned until I came here. My father told me that Zi Antonio said it was bad business to eat your own product, that that was how people lost money, that it showed a lack of respect.

I had another way of looking at it, and it was one of the reasons that I visited the sugar factory so often. In order for this to make sense, I have to describe how the sugar factory looked. Though now that I finally know what I'm *really* describing, I must admit that this might not at all have been how the factory was—just how it looked to me when I was eight years old.

Unlike any other building in our village, the factory was built of some clean, smooth material—concrete, I'd say. And it had no windows. The only way you could see inside was if you stood by the wide rear door, which I often did.

The roof of the factory was covered in pipes, sticking up toward the sky. Sometimes steam shot up from them like a volcano. When this happened, it scared me and I ran away. But I always came back.

The only times I ever stayed away for long were the few times that Zi Antonio, himself, chased me. He hardly ever came to the sugar factory, though he seemed to be everywhere else in town, including our house. As I recall, the first time he caught me, I was merely wandering about the factory yard. Out there were piles and piles of barrels just like the ones we got when we met the Palermo boat. He caught me completely by surprise. I was leaning over a row of barrels, thumping them, the way I'd seen my mother thump an eggplant to see if it was ripe. I'd just about decided that the barrels were empty, when I heard a shout close behind me. I jumped a mile. Zi Antonio towered over me like the picture of the ogre in the storybook my cousin Teresa had sent me from America. I started to cry.

Now I have to say about Zi Antonio that he always treated me and my brothers and sisters very well. "No, no, no," he said simply and shooed me away.

The second time he caught me, I was doing the same thing. The barrels seemed empty that time, too. The third time Zi Antonio said that if I continued to play there, my father would lose his job.

What I was really trying to figure out was whether the sugar in the factory was poison and whether something the men did to it made it not be poison anymore, so that when it left the factory we could eat it.

Everybody knew that Zi Antonio was the boss of the factory. We knew also that he was a special friend of the old woman who was our teacher. We knew, too, that Zi Antonio was somehow in charge of the parish church, though we assumed that must only be when the priest wasn't praying or doing holy things. Zi Antonio, for instance, was in charge of charity—being a very generous man. He was also always present at funerals, consoling the mother and the widow.

Zi Antonio was also a special friend of my mother. It was because of him, I always thought, that she took such care every Thursday when she made the sauce, for he was always our dinner guest on that night.

It was regular as the clock. All afternoon my mother would cook the sauce while my father worked at the factory. Zi Antonio would arrive. My father, being a quiet man, would say very little at the table, but Zi Antonio was funny, and his jokes kept us in stitches.

I ate faster than the others because I had to get ready to go with my father to meet the Palermo boat. I packed us a lunch. I got our sweaters and blankets. And I filled the lantern we needed to signal the big boat and let the sailors see what they were doing when they lowered the barrels into our boat.

Once in a while, a wind would arise, or the open boat would be slashed by rain, but my trust in my father was absolute. I see now that what I was doing with him was the most dangerous thing I've ever done, but I felt more safe then than I have ever felt since.

I would ask him to tell me his stories of the sea, and he always did. He knew about pirates, about explorers, about the sacred missionaries of the Church.

As we pulled away from the beach behind the sugar factory, the sun would be low over the water. I would lie against the pile of blankets as my father rowed slowly away from the village. As the last thing to fade from sight—the chimneys of the sugar factory—slipped away, the rocking of the boat would start to get to me. I would doze off. Often, the next thing I knew, I would be lying on the boat bottom staring straight up toward the stars.

Nothing in my life since has ever equaled the peace of those voyages. It seemed we drifted out there for hours. In the silence of the night, I asked my father what was in the barrels that we took from the Palermo ship into our own. He smiled and said that it was a syrup from far away, that it was needed in order to make sugar. Sugar cane? I asked him. But his eyes were trained on the water and he didn't answer.

I also asked him why nobody at the sugar factory could eat the sugar. This was a trick question. I knew, as all children do, that sometimes if you ask a question over and over again, the answer that has always been the same answer, can slip into a different answer—the truth. But he said, as he always did, that it was bad business, that it showed a lack of respect and that all the sugar in the factory belonged to Zi Antonio.

He said that Zi Antonio was the boss of the sugar factory but that he, too, had his own bosses and no matter how you lived your life, there was always somebody who had the power to tell you what to do. I didn't know what he was talking about.

I asked him why we had to wait so long. This he had explained again and again. He said that the boat to Palermo had left a country called Turkey, that when a ship was at sea, the wind could speed it or slow it, that the waves could be so high that the boat had twice as far to go—up one side, down the other. I laughed at his joke and, huddled in my warm sweater, settled back to enjoy the sandwiches I had made for us.

Often, when the boat did come, I'd been asleep, and sometimes I only woke up when I heard the shouts and saw the barrels being lowered down. Then I would fall asleep again and not wake up until our little boat reached the shore. I would crawl out onto the sand and wait there as my father rolled the barrels up into the yard of the factory. Then, he would take my hand and lead me along the path that went to our house. We'd tiptoe in, and he would tuck me into bed. Usually I was fast asleep before my door even closed, my sisters breathing silently beside me.

My memory of those nights is so vivid and complete that I remember every detail of the night that was different—the night my father was killed.

For some time before that, the arguing of my parents had been often and loud. They'd always argued, but never so much or so violently. One Thursday, my father came home from work in the middle of the afternoon. He looked different—angry and even scared. He told my mother that the sugar factory was about to close. Then, he started to drink wine. Usually, he had a little wine with his supper, but this day, he started drinking in the afternoon, which I had never seen before.

As always, my mother was cooking the sauce for supper. Despite the troubles of my father and the fact that she was fighting with him, her hands were sure as she dropped the meat into the sizzling oil. When he realized that she was making Thursday dinner as if nothing had happened at the sugar factory, he started to yell at her. How could she have Zi Antonio for dinner when he was about to ruin them all? She said Zi Antonio had nothing to do with whether the factory stayed open or closed. I had no idea what any of this meant. I was waiting for my mother to add sugar to the sauce. My father grew more and more angry. Then he stormed out of the kitchen. I ran after him, but he slammed out of the house. When I went back to the kitchen, I saw that my mother had the little cup of sugar resting on the cupboard. I stepped up, stuck out my finger and reached up to coat it with sugar. To my amazement, my mother slapped my hand so hard that I hit it on the edge of the cupboard and cut it. She didn't even offer to help me. She told me to get out, to wash it off, and to come right back. I did everything she said. A little later, my father came back and went into my parents' room, where he remained.

Zi Antonio did come for supper that night, but there were no jokes. He wasn't even hungry. All we ate was salad, cheese and bread. He and my mother whispered as we all sat at the table. I thought they were whispering to keep from waking my father who had fallen asleep after drinking all that wine. I kept waiting for my father to wake up, for us to go out to the boat. But every time I tried to get up from the table, my mother told me to sit down.

After a long time, my father did wake up, but I knew it was too late for us to go out. It was already dark. My mother now seemed a lot less angry than she'd been. She had even put aside some sauce for my father, and she cooked him macaroni and ladled the sauce onto it. He, too, must have been over his anger, because I could see how hungry he was. He ate it all. Then he went back into the room he shared with my mother, stretched out across the bed and fell back to sleep.

I was heartbroken. All day I'd thought about our trip out to the Palermo boat, and now, clearly, we weren't going. I went to bed myself.

But I had a hard time sleeping. In the middle of the night, I got up to ask my parents if I could get in bed with them until I fell asleep. I crept down the hall. Their door was open, and I looked in. They were lying side by side. A broad ray of moonlight fell straight across my father's face. He had told me again and again that it was bad luck to sleep in the moonlight. Here he was, sound asleep, completely unprotected from the moon. But even more disturbing was the sight of my mother. The moonlight fell on her face, too. She was not asleep. Her eyes were wide open, staring straight up and full of tears that fell down her face, sparkling like diamonds in the pale light.

I knew then that she was sorry they had fought. I knew, too, that their room was no place for me. I went back to my own room and fell asleep.

Things happened very fast after that. The next day, my father couldn't wake up. The doctor came. Then the priest. He was dead before either got there. They said it was the shock of knowing that the factory was going to close. They said he must always have had a weak heart. They said it was such a shame—a man in his thirties with five children....

Zi Antonio saved us. He told my mother that he would look after us all. He said that his bosses had decided to send him to Canada. He said we could all go with him. My mother wore black clothes all the way to Canada. We had stopped in Rome to get them.

After we got to the new country, our lives settled down. It was strange at first to have Zi Antonio with us every day, instead of one day a week. It was strange to have a father—he and my mother soon married—who worked in an office every day instead of a factory. And it was strange to live in a real city instead of a village. But there were so many good things—the school, the museum, the parks, the friends. Before long, I forgot about Sicily. I never, of course, forgot about my father. But it hurt to think of him dying at such a young age. He had been my friend. Now I had other friends. And after a while, I hardly thought about him at all.

Zi Antonio offered to send me to university, but I was rebellious. When I left school, I, like my father, went to work in a factory. It was clean work. If you paid attention and worked quickly, you could make good money. I started at the machines, sewing pajamas. I soon moved up to hand-stitching dresses, and then, I became one of the senior women. At the time I left, I had been making the finest wedding gowns, beading lace that cost five hundred dollars per meter.

After many years, the orders started to fall off because of the dresses from China. One by one the women had to be let go. Finally, there were only four of us left—the wedding women. Every day for two years, I had gone in thinking it would be my last day, and one day it was. The boss was crying. She didn't even have the money to give us a settlement. The last thing she did was pay the wages she owed us. That was it.

Except for the counsellor. The boss gave a little speech about how the government had provided counselling for us all. We could learn to write resumes. We could explore retraining. We could learn creative writing—to get in touch with our inner selves, she said.

What could my resume say? That I had been sewing for thirty years? For what could I retrain? And I had already taken a writing course from the government.

The only program left was "Looking into Ourselves." So it was this workshop that I signed up for, this workshop in which I discovered the secret I had been keeping from my "inner self" all my life.

It happened so simply and so suddenly. I went to the community center where the workshop was to be held. At first everyone was nervous and embarrassed. But it was all women and pretty soon we started to chat. As the weeks went by, I started to feel comfortable talking to the women in the group, who ranged in age from a little younger than me to a little older.

One night, there were some young women there—all sitting together and so pretty, the way my mother was the day she left our village to come to Canada with my step-father.

One of these girls told us that she went to a different group every night in order to never have to spend an evening alone. The silence was total as she told us in a shaky voice that she had been a drug addict.

Now of course, for women my age, to have a granddaughter on drugs is the ultimate terror. I had even gone to a lecture once about all the different drugs and the history of where they came from, sponsored by the police.

The girl spoke only a little—laughing and crying as she told us about herself. What she said was that the first time she ever saw heroin, it looked just like sugar. That it sparkled and she had put out her finger and taken a little and tasted it, expecting it to be sweet, but it was bitter. And that should have told her all she needed to know.

I saw it then. I saw the whole thing. I saw my father lifting up his arms to receive the barrels of opium from Turkey—just like the police told us about. I saw the factory with its frightening pipes and its strange white product that no one was allowed to eat. I saw Zi Antonio with his fine suits, with the respect, the fear of everyone in our village. And I saw my mother slipping a silk blouse out of a shiny paper bag from Rome.

I picked up my coat and my purse and I walked out of the center and all the way home.

But even then, I had only figured out part of it. It took me until far into the night before I realized what Zi Antonio and my mother were doing every Thursday night. And then, most cruelly of all, I remembered my mother's sharp anger the day I watched her put the secret ingredient into her famous sauce. The day I reached out my finger to taste the sugar as I had done so many times before.

I was sick the next day. All day I dreamed about my childhood. By the time my husband came home, I could no longer tell what was a dream and what was reality.

Perhaps next week, I'll return to the group. I'll tell them I'm still depressed about losing my job, that I feel tired all the time, that I'm afraid a woman my age can never find work again. But I'll never speak about my mother. To whom would I tell her story and why? From the day we came to Canada, we lived a law-abiding life. We went to school, then we worked, then we married and sent our own children to school. Zi Antonio died, and so did my mother. My children have never much wanted to know about the old country.

No, I am the only one remaining who knows the secret of Zi Antonio and my mother. The night I looked in and saw my father so very still that the moonlight on his face could not wake him, I took this secret to myself, without even knowing. Now, because of a few troubled words, I do know. But the secret stays with me. It floats in my mind, detached from all else, the way our little boat floated—a small speck on the waters that lapped the shore of our tiny village, spilled onward toward the bay of Palermo, crossed the Mediterranean, then slipped out to the real sea.

Rosemary Aubert has achieved world-wide attention with her Ellis Portal series. She is a Toronto writer, teacher, speaker and criminologist who mentors fresh mystery writers and treasures classic ones.

About the Author

After a successful career as an internationally-published romance writer, Rosemary Aubert turned to the world of crime, graduating with a Certificate of Criminology from the University of Toronto and publishing the six-volume award-winning, Ellis Portal mystery series. Rosemary also worked in the real world of crime. She was a security officer at the United States Consulate. She ran the office of a half-way house for men leaving the federal prison system. She served as a Community Relations director assisting women coming out of the prison system. And for ten years, she was a bailiff in the criminal courts.

These experiences introduced Rosemary to a wide variety of people—innocent and guilty, dangerous and safe. These denizens of the real world of crime inspired the characters that inhabit The Midnight Boat to Palermo.

Born in Niagara Falls, New York, Rosemary has long made her home in Toronto, where she has worked as a university instructor, an editor and a bookstore clerk and of course—a writer.

www.ingramcontent.com/pod-product-compliance
Lightning Source LLC
Chambersburg PA
CBHW020910180626
46816CB00007BA/2326